THE LONGEST SPEED DATE

THE WILDE SISTERS DUET
BOOK 2

LOUISA DUVAL

Ballydoon Books
PO Box 1033
Oxley QLD 4075
Australia
https://louisaduval.com

First published in Australia by Ballydoon Books in 2024.

Book Cover Design and Illustration by Ivanna Nashkolna (Instagram: @i.nashkolna)

Proofreading by Jo Speirs at Nurturing Words

First edition: February 2024

Ebook: 978-0-6455600-1-5

Print: 978-0-6455600-4-6

❀ Created with Vellum

For every woman who has had a man slide into their DMs.
May his dirty talk game be as good as Jethro.

ACKNOWLEDGMENTS

Jenny and Keith Gordan out at Longreach: They run a sheep station and talked to me about their life, how the sheep are shorn and the realities of living on the land.
And Sue Jarman, our old neighbour: Lots of talk about animals, including sheep, ponies and dogs. Captain Sook is still going strong.
Hope I did you all proud.

Neva: for sharing the horror stories as well as the highlights of speed dating nights. Thank you so much for sharing and for asking your friends for their stories, too!

Brutus Cookie Clan, especially Ariane: thank you for letting me use your name. You're a lioness in the pursuit of happiness! May you find your Jethro.

Maureen: my favourite Canadian, who pointed out zebra is like zeeee-bra in North America. But technically, y'all Canucks were taught it's zeh-bra, like Debra!

Danièle: for the record, beetroot is delicious, but I channelled your hatred for this story.

READER NOTE:

This story has steamy heat, uses Aussie slang, has swearing, and the couple has a hard-won, guaranteed HEA.
You should also know that zebra is pronounced z-eh-bra here in Australia. Not zee-bra.
Debra Wilde, thank you in advance.
Now, let's get ready to fall in love, one question at a time!

1

Ari

True confessions: Do you believe in love at first sight?

"You might meet someone special tonight, sweetie," Mum trilled as I placed the last pack of conversation starter cards on a table for the Ballydoon Speed Dating Night.

Ugh, gag.

"For a woman who taught her daughters, and I quote, 'men will always be the ruin of the Wilde women' since our father walked out on us, why are you organising a speed dating night?"

"Cody, of course, sweetie."

"Okay, fine. Mr Golden Retriever from Canada is the exception."

Cody had swept my sister, Ash, off her feet in a whirlwind romance. And he was a good guy. Kind of wonderful, actually.

"I've had complete about-face on the topic of love." Mum taped the last of the bunting to the football plaque on the dining room wall. "My dear Ari, love is something everyone needs."

Double gag.

"Even you."

"Nope, I'm good. Thanks."

I swatted a paper love heart out of my eyes. Love was literally in the air tonight. I pulled the bunting tighter so it didn't hit others in the face as they walked into the room.

Mum's taste in party decorations could only be described as 'Cupid vomit'. Bunting and balloons hung over tables covered in pink, red and white tablecloths, with glitter love heart sprinkles and a battery-operated candle in the centre. A red and white balloon arch greeted guests at the door.

"I don't want anyone special, Mum. I just want to get laid."

Mum pointedly ignored my declaration with a dramatic sigh as she laid out her paperwork on the registration table, and then pursed her lips. "Have you had a chance to rethink this road trip of yours?"

But more than my hate about the Cult of Falling in Love was my frustration with Mum trying to shoehorn me into a job I didn't want.

"Mum. I. Am. Not. Joining. Your. Salon."

She *tsked* under her breath. "You had a vibrant career in film in Sydney, and you could easily have a vibrant career here in Ballydoon and the surrounding district with wedding make-up—"

"Mum, enough!"

She fell silent with a *harrumph*. Her phone rang, and

finally, she was distracted from my career woes and man troubles.

Sydney, the whole film and TV industry and wedding make-up could all just get in the bin.

Dating an actor from the hit show *Thousand Acres of Dust* sounded vibrant. Exciting, even.

At the time my sister announced she was in love with Cody, my then-boyfriend and TV star, Wes Schumacher, had stomped on my heart and kicked it to the curb in the worst possible way.

Even calling him my ex-boyfriend was a stretch. Everything about our relationship had been a lie. We'd never been public with our relationship—affair—whatever you'd call it in hindsight. Never went out with our colleagues or friends.

Not anything remotely like this speed date night. Not even a date, speedy or slow.

I'd done his make-up on set and in private, he'd ... done me. So to speak.

Not that I thought we were having an affair. Ever. I'd thought I'd been in love.

"People will be arriving soon," Mum called out from the registration table, rousing me from my thoughts.

I slapped the last set of cards on a table, and I had to admit it, Mum had done a great job. "I might not believe in love, but you outdid yourself with the cards."

Mum had made cards and called the pack 'Date Night Questions', complete with a cupcake and a chili for sweet and spicy questions.

"Thank you. I'm rather impressed myself."

"Just how spicy are some of these questions?" I picked one up at random and read it aloud. "Have you ever used sex toys with a partner or by yourself?" I let the card fall to the table with a squeal. "Mum! You can't ask locals that!"

"Whyever not?" Mum placed the card back in the pack, thankfully in the middle. "I never thought you a prude, Ari."

"I'm not ... it's just ... That's a very intimate thing to ask someone you have just met."

"Exploration with toys in the bedroom is far more acceptable nowadays."

Ryan, the bartender, stopped in his tracks before us. "Um. Ah ... drinks, ladies?"

"Wine spritzer, thank you, Ryan." Mum trundled off, leaving me alone with him.

"Another white wine. Thanks."

Ryan darted away as quickly as he could. What other bloody questions had she done? Maybe I should have checked before she had them printed.

"Just give tonight a chance. Before you decide to drive off into the sunset in Cody's Kombi van and leave your mother here alone in Ballydoon."

A week ago, after three glasses of wine, I'd decided I was going on a road trip around Australia with what little money I had and Cody's Kombi van which he'd sold to me for a bargain price. An odyssey of self-discovery. See the country and find myself.

At least, that's what #vanlyf looked like on Instagram.

And I'd had an epiphany. There was one thing I needed to do before I left on my road trip: rebound sex.

I needed to get Wes out of my system. And by that, I meant sleep with someone: a one-night stand.

"Ari, you sit there. People are arriving." Mum inhaled a deep breath and then clapped. "Get ready to fall in love, one question at a time!"

I groaned, dutifully sitting down at the table she had

pointed at. Ryan placed my wine before me, and I took a grateful sip.

The 'Ballydoon Pub Speed Dating Night' was the perfectly timed event to pick-up for rebound sex, even with Mum as the event's hostess and her dreams of fairytale happily ever afters.

But I'd never propositioned a guy. Ever.

Wes had been the flirt and asked me out. And we'd only seen each other at my place, never his. Sometimes at work in his trailer. Never public, never photographed together.

Until the day I'd showed up to surprise him.

And instead, he surprised me in the worst possible way.

I sipped my wine again. My second glass for the night. I made a mental note to sneak off during the event's break, where we were supposed to mingle with each other, and get some hot chips from the kitchen. A perk of having your sister also working behind the bar at the Ballydoon pub.

And, I mean, seriously: what man is better than hot chips and gravy?

Anyway, alcohol and I did not have a great working relationship on an empty stomach despite recent wine-induced epiphanies.

I could do this. Before meeting Cody, Ash had made picking up men look easy. She'd only have to look at them a certain way and they'd be lining up for her attention. Before Cody, her motto had been 'here for a short time, not a long time'. Up until Cody, Mum believed men were the ruin of us all.

I could blame Cody for everyone in my family believing in true love, but the thing was, he was so damn nice. Ash was a lucky girl. He was the exception.

I snorted and swallowed a large gulp of my wine. *Happily ever afters can just get in the bin.*

"I am a woman of destiny who can ask a man for a night of no-strings sex," I muttered to the tabletop.

I straightened my shoulders and smoothed my knit top, one shoulder bare, leaving it clear that I was wearing a strapless bra. My top clung to me in a way that begged attention. My skinny jeans, heeled boots, hair in loose waves over my other shoulder and a little smoky eye completed my look.

I was ready. Let's do this.

Half an hour later, after the start, more women than men were here. I sat at my table alone with my wine, waiting for the bell to ring and the men to move on to another table to meet other women.

So far, I'd met two guys, and I'd forgotten their names already. Cardigan Guy had talked about the complexities of tax laws in Australia and given me a coupon if I needed help with my tax return. Zero attraction.

The second man was Hardware Store Guy. He'd stared at the tablecloth while answering my awkward questions 'What's your favourite colour?' grunting 'green' and 'What do you like to read?' with 'I don't'. Another hard pass.

I'd set up a Tinder profile just before I'd left Sydney, my career and Wes Schumacher, but hadn't used it to pick up someone swiping this way and that. I was about to give up on Mum's speed dating night and head home when thunder rumbled, shaking the building. Everyone tittered and 'ooohed' as a guy walked in at the same time lightning lit up the doorway. He brushed raindrops from his fringe and introduced himself to Mum at the registration table.

Droplets clung to his forearms which flexed, doing very sexy, muscly things. He leant down, placing a motorbike helmet and a leather jacket on the floor, his jeans hugging his butt and thighs. His black AC/DC tee shirt was stretched across his chest. His biceps looked strong enough to bench press me. Two of me.

Arm Porn. My skin tingled from my scalp to my toes.

He was nothing like Wes. *Perfect for a night of rebound sex.*

He was in a different league to every man here. A fantastically ripped league.

I gulped a large mouthful of wine. *Shit, I must get something to eat ...*

Mum handed him the speed dating scorecard we'd all received to tick off who we liked during the event, and then she laughed. "Call me Debra! Like zebra." Mum leant into him, squeezing his forearm. "Not Debbie or Deb-*bor*-rah. Deb. Ra." She let him go, breathing, "Oh my!" and then pointed to me. "Ariane Wilde is free right now at that table over there. But let's get your details first."

I looked away, straightening my back, and downed the rest of my wine to drown my nerves. *I can do this,* I chanted in my mind for the thousandth time. *I'm a sexually independent woman who can ask a man for casual sex.*

Ryan caught my eye from the bar and tipped his chin in a universal gesture of 'another?' I nodded vigorously.

A bell rang, and the men swapped tables, still leaving me alone. Some of the women went to the bar for another drink as the next round started. I shuffled the date night cards to distract myself. Thank goodness the sex toys question hadn't randomly been chosen with Cardigan Guy or Hardware Store Guy.

I'd asked Cardigan Guy what his ideal first date was, and he'd launched into a monologue about cost-effective dates, including no-cost alternatives for the budget-conscious. I wasn't a high-maintenance woman who wanted high-end restaurants, or clubs, or expensive bars.

I just wanted to be seen.

I jumped when Ryan appeared with another glass of white wine. "Added it to your tab. Just pay at the end, Ari."

I thanked him, placed the cards on the table and took a sip.

"You're braver than I am, attending a night like this." Ryan brushed a love heart from his face as he cleared an empty table beside me.

I chuckled. "I am questioning my life choices right now." I glanced to Arm Porn who was paying the registration fee with his credit card. "I think Mum's hoping I'll meet a nice young man who will talk me out of my road trip around Australia. Tonight is Operation Insta-Love."

"Ha. Heard that you bought Cody's Kombi. Happy to check it over before your big trip if you like."

Ryan worked three jobs: with Ash as bar staff on weekends until she started her promotion as a line order cook for the pub's bistro. During the week, he worked at Turner's Mechanical as a mechanic as well as running his family's historic sheep station just outside of Ballydoon.

"Oh yes, good idea. Thank you."

Ryan turned to walk away and hesitated. "And, ah, sorry to hear about Wes. Your mum mentioned you'd split up with him."

Everyone knew Wes from his TV show, and everyone knew everyone's business in Ballydoon.

"I'm fine." I grimaced, clearly sounding not fine. "I'm moving on."

"Hope you're not going anywhere just yet." Arm Porn was standing beside my table, smiling. He then offered his hand to Ryan. "G'day, I'm Jet. Jethro Cummings." As they shook hands, Jet glanced my way as if sizing me up, and then winked. "That's right. Plural."

My eyebrows slowly rose.

Ryan coughed, his eyes widening briefly before he asked Jet for his drink order and then hastily retreated.

I swallowed hard. *You can do it. You have eight minutes. Just ask him.* Jet draped his jacket over the back of his chair and then took his seat.

His cheeks were flushed, and he didn't look me in the eye. "Umm, nice to meet you, Ariane."

"It's Ari."

"Ari. Right." He licked his lips and took the first two cards from the pack. "What do you prefer, sweet or spicy?"

He smiled, his grey-blue eyes sparkling with a mix of sex and sin.

Or maybe that's my wine filter. Was he nervous?

Time to cut to the chase. "No cards," I blurted. "I only have one question."

"Alright, ask away."

"I need a man who knows how to fuck." Both of his eyebrows shot up. I continued, clutching my wine to stop my hands from shaking. "I want one night of multiple orgasms, minimum of two. I'm leaving in two days on a big trip around Australia so no strings attached and no awkward running into each other afterwards, trying to make small talk. I just want a night of great sex before I leave."

I paused, sucking on my bottom lip, to summon the courage I needed to ask one question.

"So, Jethro Cummings, my question is, are you the man for the job?"

2

Jet

Spicy question: Have you played with toys in the bedroom with a partner? With yourself?

The cards in my hand fell to the table.

The question about sex toys sat on top of the pile. I slapped my hand down like I was playing Snap.

What kind of night was this?

A second passed. Then two. Three.

I'd just been asked to have sex with a hot woman. After using that awful pick-up line.

And she was serious.

My gaze settled on her full lips as I contemplated the possibility of spending the night with her. I shifted in my seat, my jeans now uncomfortable.

"Did you talk to Blake?" I hedged.

Ari frowned. "Who the hell is Blake?" She titled her head. "Do you want to have sex or not?"

She was serious. I didn't even have to get through the cards and she was good to go for sex. Just like that.

And then I sighed.

The answer was no.

"This was not how it was supposed to go." I groaned. My best mate Blake would be on the floor laughing if he was witnessing this right now.

"Erm, *what?*" Ari looked horrified.

I held up my hands. "No, I mean that line about my last name." Ari frowned. "Jethro *Cummings*? Anyway, I'd bet my mate, Blake, I would absolutely get shot down and roasted for that lame joke about my name and I'd collect twenty dollars off him."

"A *bet?*" she spat.

"No! Yes, I mean no!" I scrubbed my face. "The bet was stupid because of, well, my last name. I'm here because ... I wanted to meet someone."

Ari snorted. "Were you expecting to find true love at a speed dating night at a country pub?"

"Maybe." I avoided her eyes, looking around the room. *Pfft ... yes, I was.* "I'm tired of casual hook ups. I travel a lot for work, only staying for a few weeks, a couple of months tops, in each place. And now, something more permanent has come up."

Ari stared at me intently, and yeah, I noticed how her eyes lingered on my arms. "What do you do?" she asked, finally looking up.

"Contract shearing. Used to travelling all over following the work but ..." I still found it hard to talk about, even though the paperwork went through two weeks ago. "I've just inherited my late grandfather's farm. Had no idea he was leaving the place to me and my brother. My bro has no interest in farming, so I'm buying him out. Never in a million years thought I'd own a house or land, or both. Keen to get it running as a small sheep farm, a mix of wool and meat. So I'm kinda a farmer, and sometimes a shearer. And now that I'm not on the road anymore, I'd like to meet someone special."

Ari nodded, completely unfazed by my rambling. I was about to ask her what she did for a crust when she shook her head. "Less than five hundred people live in Ballydoon so statistics are against you finding someone here. Wait." Her cherry-red lips formed a perfect O. "Oh my God, do you *actually* believe in love?"

I burst out laughing. "That's what you concluded from what I said?"

Ari snorted again. Somehow, it was cute how she did it.

I shrugged. "I just want to have a meaningful relation-ship, you know?"

She rolled her eyes. I was floundering. "You don't believe in love?"

"I tried 'love'." Ari made quotation marks in the air, her voice dripping with disdain. "For two years, and it left me broke, unemployed, back at home, and—" She leant across the table. "Unsatisfied."

I blinked slowly. "Heard the bar guy say you'd just broken up with someone." I glanced towards the bar where —what was his name again? Ryan, that's it—was wiping it down. *Better remember Ryan's name in two days' time.* "Guy called Wes Schumacher?"

"A month ago." Ari shuddered.

A thought occurred to me. "Isn't he on that show on TV?"

"*Thousand Acres of Dust*, yeah. Met him on the set. I'm a make-up artist." She scowled. "Was a make-up artist." She blinked, her eyes glassy, then blushed. "Caught him having sex with another woman. He was my first." Ari blinked again and huffed out a laugh. "Sweet baby cheeses! If I was going to make confessions all night, I would have fronted up at the church instead of speed dating at the pub."

I kept my face neutral. Ari wasn't seething with rage or dealing with a broken heart. If anything, she looked embarrassed. Ashamed.

"I'm really sorry that happened," I whispered. "Your ex did a real number on you, didn't he?"

Ari blinked rapidly, like she was about to cry. *Shit, Jet: first, you shoot down an offer of sex, and then you back it up by making her cry.*

"I'm sorry. Can I get you napkins or something?"

She ignored me, swigging the rest of the wine, her glass making a dull *thunk* on our table. "Well, thank you for your pity, but I'll just move on and ask someone else to have sex with me."

A throat cleared. We both looked up to find Ryan holding my beer. He placed it in front of me and took off without a word.

Ari's words hit me as I took a sip of the lager.

"Wait, you're just going to ask some random stranger here tonight for sex?" I hissed.

"Yeah, why not? I just did with you."

"Well, yes, but ..." I leant forward. "How do you know if you can trust him?"

"Trust him to deliver on at least two orgasms?"

"No, I mean if he's a creep!" I paused. "Wes never gave you two orgasms? Ever?"

What was wrong with this guy? Ari was pretty. Really pretty. How did this Wes guy not want to see how many times he could make her ...

I shifted in my seat. Things were uncomfortable again in my jeans.

"I never experienced that with Wes." She blushed. "My ex-workmates in Sydney used to talk about how their boyfriends or lovers gave them multiples. I used to wonder if others were making up their stories about multiple orgasms, but my sister confirmed she definitely does with her fiancé."

Hang on a sec ... "You've *never* had more than one orgasm with guys other than Wes too?"

"Wes was my first"—she took a deep breath—"and only lover."

My eyebrows rose.

"I just need to know if something's wrong with me because ... I know Wes was capable of doing it more than once because... because ... *shit*. On the day I caught them, first I heard them like they were both close to coming. Lots of 'oh Gods' and 'yes, yes' sort of thing." She shuddered. "Then, I noticed the used condom on a pile of tissues on the floor as I walked through the door to then find him ... and her ... *climaxing*. They came together as I stood there, wanting to stab my eyes out with a fork! She got multiples, and I never did!"

Out of the corner of my eye, I saw other speed-dating couples staring at us. "Ignore them." I waved a hand, catching her attention. "This Wes guy is a total douchebag."

"Thanks. He was. Still is. At least I know I'm not into watching others do it." She laughed without humour as she picked up her wineglass and sipped nothing but air. "Well, fuck."

Her glass landed on the table with another loud *thunk*.

"I just want to know what it's like with another guy. I

want one night of rebound sex so I can move on and make my way in the world. I just ... yeah."

Her eyes slowly blinked as they roamed around the room. Far out, was she sizing up the other candidates for sex? Who knew which of the guys were utter creeps and who was decent?

She deserved better than what Wes had done to her. No woman deserved what Wes had done to Ari.

My jaw ticked. "Okay."

Where the hell had that come from?

"Okay, what?" she asked, slowly blinking again.

"Okay, I'll do it." I tipped my chin. "Sleep with you. Tonight." *Holy shit.*

Ari slowly blinked again, biting her lip as she grabbed her clutch. "You mean it? You're going to sleep with me?"

"That's right." I stood, leant over the table and held her gaze. "After I'm done with you, you won't have any memories of your ex in bed."

Ari stood up, giggling, a little unsteady on her feet.

"Let's go have orgasms!" she exclaimed, punching the air.

What the fuck have I got myself into?

3

Ari

Surf or turf: Do you prefer the mountains or the beach for a weekend getaway?

I sat up and instantly regretted my first decision for the day. My head was pounding, and I couldn't quite figure out which way was up or down.

I'd drank too much—again—on an empty stomach. At five foot four, I was a lightweight with alcohol, and I'd been an idiot last night to drink without food.

Somehow, I'd made it to my temporary home, walking three streets to my Kombi van parked in Ash's backyard, and fell asleep here.

Hazy memories formed: someone carrying me, me singing AC/DC's 'You Shook Me All Night Long' badly, my mother giggling in the background, yelling at my make-up kits and brush sets about how I hated being a make-up artist, throwing clothes around the van.

I inhaled a steadying breath. Three things occurred to me at once: One, I'd not paid for my tab. Two, the tee shirt I was wearing was *not* mine.

And three, despite asking that guy with the really nice arms for a night of sex, I did *not* feel like I'd had sex all night.

I sniffed the tee shirt I was wearing, and oh my God, whoever owned this, they smelled good.

And then I groaned. A tornado had ripped through my clothing, leaving my shirts and underwear on every surface and handle. A tornado called Drunk Ari.

My mouth had turned into cotton wool. I pushed my hair to the side and saw that someone had left painkillers and a glass of water on the van's kitchen bench.

Thoughtful of Mum.

I looked back down at the black tee I wore. AC/DC on the front. The same band tee shirt Jet had worn to speed dating.

Jet Cummings: that's right, plural!

Who had agreed to have sex with me.

I whipped up the shirt. My strapless bra was gone, but I was still wearing my black lace briefs I'd worn to speed dating. I tensed my core muscles. Definitely did *not* feel like I'd seen any action last night.

Someone started humming a song outside at the back of the van. A very masculine-sounding someone.

I swallowed the pills and the whole glass of water, and then peeked out the rear window. Jet was shirtless and lying on the ground with some spanners at his side, swearing at my muffler.

Okay, this was most unexpected. I pulled back from the window. I'd gone to the pub looking to hook-up, and the Kombi had ended up with more lube than I did.

My Kombi van. Still wasn't used to the fact that I now owned a vintage campervan. Shit, I wasn't even used to the idea that Ash—'here for a good time, not a long time'—Wilde was happily in love, that Mum was now acting as the official matchmaker of Ballydoon, and I was doing a road trip of the whole of Australia.

Did you need lube for a muffler? Why is Jet touching my Kombi van? In fact, why was he still here? I gritted my teeth, shuffled off the bed, slid the heavy sliding door across with a bang and whimpered at the bright light. I looked around, finding my sunnies on top of my make-up kit, and put them on as I charged outside.

"What do you think you're doing?" I screamed and immediately winced as my voice clanged in my skull. *Come on, drugs, do your thing!*

Jet put down a spanner and sat up slowly, looking me up and down. "Well, good morning."

Fuck, I ran out here in nothing but my panties and his shirt! From his seated position on the ground, his eyes were level with my underwear. I pulled the hem of his tee shirt down a little.

"How's your head?" he asked, his voice low and deep.

"Like Thor is taking his hammer to my skull."

"You find the painkillers and water?"

"I did. You left those out for me?"

He nodded.

"Thank you," I said in a small voice.

"No problem." Jet smiled. "Thought you might need them after last night."

Panic pulsed through me. I'd just taken pills from a stranger. That I picked up in a bar. That I had kinda blacked out on. I was the biggest idiot on this planet. No, this galaxy! All of the galaxies!

"You okay?" Jet got to his feet, his brow furrowed with concern. "You look like you're going to puke."

"What are you doing?" I demanded.

Jet waved to my muffler. "I was awake, and you'd rolled off me, so I got up and let you sleep. Checked out the Kombi and the muffler was loose. She's a classic. So many original features on her."

"Her?"

"Yeah, Kombis are definitely girls. What's her name?"

"She—*it*—doesn't have a name."

"*She* needs a name."

"I've been more concerned with planning my trip, and I haven't had time to think of a name—"

Jet turned to the van and considered the orange and white paint job and chrome bumper. An ancient, faded sticker clung to the back window in defiance of its age: a corgi with 'sassy butt' written underneath.

I openly stared as his arms flexed when he wiped sweat from his brow. Sweat beaded on his chest and his arms. One bead of sweat almost followed the swirls and pattern of this tattoos as it made its way down. I may have had a hangover, but I hadn't forgotten just how much I wanted to lick those arms last night.

Jet clicked his fingers. "Bessie."

"Huh?" I asked, reluctantly lifting my gaze from his biceps to look him in the eye.

"Bessie. Definitely."

"Who? The van?"

"Yep. For sure."

"That's a ridiculous name. Hey, are these my tools?" I bent down to pick up a spanner and turned around to face him and caught Jet checking out my butt. I stamped my foot. "Excuse me! You can't just make yourself at home here.

You're a complete stranger and—" I gulped as dread washed over me. "Fuck, you warned me about picking up complete strangers last night, didn't you?"

Jet nodded. "What else do you remember, Ari?"

"I ... ah ... said I was getting orgasms, and then ... It's blurry after that." My cheeks were burning up.

"You almost fell to the floor when we got up to leave."

"Oh God, the wine! I only had three." My hand flew to my stomach. "I forgot to eat." My hand then flew to my forehead. "And I didn't pay my tab!"

"I took care of it. Ryan had to cover the speed dating night while Debra helped me get you home. I pretty much carried you here. And don't worry, you used the bathroom by yourself and drank some water. And you didn't puke."

It's a special kind of relief when you're reassured you hadn't peed your pants or puked over yourself.

"Mum just let you come to the house?" I balled up my fists. "I'm going to kill her when I see her! But ..." I paused, looking down my front. "Why am I wearing your tee shirt?" I pointed the spanner at his chest to keep some distance between us. At his impressively broad, bare, glistening chest.

"First, I don't think Debra could've carried you by herself. And second, you basically did a strip show. I chased you around the van to put a shirt on, but you refused every tee shirt you own and threw them everywhere." Jet paused, and his cheeks pinked. "And yes, I saw your tits." His eyes strayed down to my chest as he murmured, "Bloody great tits."

His eyes snapped back up to mine, and he cleared his throat. "I swear I was nothing but a gentleman last night, but it's really hard not to notice your breasts when you were topless. The only shirt you would agree to wear was mine."

I crossed my arms. "So last night, did we ... you know?"

"No, *no!* Ari. I would never—" He waved his hands and then sighed. "I'm not that kind of guy. Shit. I promise you, I'm not an arsehole! You can check with Debra about how I updated her with texts about you after she went back to the speed dating night."

"She just left me with you?" My jaw fell open.

"Ari, you demanded I stay with you until you fell asleep."

"How do I know you didn't cop a feel when I was out of it?"

"Oh, Ari, that's all on you last night." He took a step towards me, his eyes turning from earnest to fiery in an instant. "Your hands wander when you're drunk."

"I beg your pardon!"

How dare he! Jet took another step forward. I dropped the spanner and backed away but found myself up against Bessie. *I mean the van.*

"You slept on me last night," he said in a low voice. "You would only settle if you were sprawled across my chest, and as to your hands, they—" He paused to lick his lips. "They kept travelling south."

"You're lying," I whispered, horrified.

Jet raised one eyebrow. "You kept saying you wanted to touch my Wonder Dick."

'Wonder Dick' triggered a memory: me tracking my hand down his happy trail, moaning, *"But I wanna touch your Wonder Dick!"* and Jet catching my hand, laughing, telling me to go to sleep.

I pressed a hand to my burning forehead, my stomach roiling. "I'm so sorry. I was not myself last night. That's not an excuse. Sorry."

"The ex, Wes."

I nodded and then shook it. "Wes isn't an excuse either. Nor is too much wine on an empty stomach. I'm a lightweight, and I was an idiot for not eating. Why would you still be here after how I behaved?"

"Thought I made it clear I'm not an arsehole, Ari." Jet frowned. "I stayed to make sure you were okay, and, well, I fell asleep too. I swear you're a human blanket because you'd only sleep if you were on top of me. I ended up trapped."

I snorted, my eyes falling on his biceps. We both knew he was not trapped under five foot four, little ol' me.

My stomach growled. He dusted his hands off and headed to the van's door.

"Breakfast? I know you've got eggs, six slices of bread and a dribble of milk in your fridge. Could make French toast, if you like. Then I'll head off."

"You cook?"

"No need to sound so surprised. And you should have enough milk for coffee too. If you have coffee. I searched and couldn't find any."

My stomach groaned again. "You can wash up in the house," I offered weakly.

The least I could do was let him use a tap and some soap.

"Got bathroom sorted. And kitchen. Your sister showed me."

Of course Ash did. My jaw fell open. How easily he'd made himself at home while I'd been sleeping off the wine.

"Or I can leave now." Jet then grinned. "But I'd need my shirt back. If you'd like to just take it off?"

I hugged myself and sniffed. "Breakfast would be nice. And coffee is in the house."

He smirked and strode towards the back door.

"Hey, Jet." He looked at me over his shoulder. "Thank you. For last night."

"Anytime, Ari." He smiled and disappeared into the house.

4

Ari

Cupcake: What is the meaning behind your name?

I groaned under the stream of hot water in the shower, scrubbing away the sourness of last night's wine. As I washed my hair with Ash's shampoo, something occurred to me. There was no way Jet could have been shown around the house by my sister. Cody had taken her for a weekend getaway at the beach.

They'd left yesterday morning.

I'd caught Jet out with his lie.

The smell of eggs and butter wafted under the door as I turned off the water. I was out in two minutes, hair wrapped in a towel and ready to eat—and confront him.

Jet was now wearing a tee shirt from a Canadian ice hockey team—one of Cody's.

"That belongs to Cody."

"Your sister said it was okay." He flipped the French toast in a skillet.

"My sister is away with Cody."

Jet frowned. "But Debra was here this morning when I got up."

Oh, Mum. "What? Debra is not my sister. She's my mum."

"Your *mum*?" He almost dropped the second slice of French toast, his eyes wide. "Debra said she was your older sister!"

"You actually believed her? I can't believe she just let you into my real sister's house. Oh my God!"

He threw back his head and groaned. I tried not to think about how much I liked that sound.

"To be fair, I was very busy catching you from hitting the pavement rather than judging if your sister was old enough to be your mother." He sighed, pulling at Cody's tee. "Would you prefer I didn't wear this? Debra did say I could have it."

Cody was broad across the shoulders, and somehow, Jet managed to stretch the tee shirt further. I licked my lips, contemplating the idea of having Shirtless Jet serve me breakfast, then shook my head.

"I'm sure it's fine." I gulped down several mouthfuls of water. "I am totally going to kill her and bury her in this yard. Turn her into compost for the veggie patch!"

"You take hangry to a whole new murdery vibe, Ari." He held up a plate of French toast. "Whereas, I'm going to deal with the mortification of someone's mum letting her drunk daughter go home with a random dude by eating this excellent breakfast."

Jet sprinkled parsley on my French toast. He'd even cut up some tomatoes to go with it. He smiled sheepishly, holding a plate right under my nose. "Care to join me?"

I groaned. "You sprinkled cheese on one side and fried it?"

"Of course." He smirked, his voice low again.

It was a known fact that if anyone wanted to kidnap me, all they'd need to do was leave a trail of cheese and I'd follow the trail all the way to the kidnapper's lair.

I followed Jet as if under a spell to the kitchen table, where his leather jacket was draped over a chair. I sat beside him, and we ate in silence.

Jet finished first and placed something on the table between us. "Does your name have a special meaning? If so, what is it?"

I gave him the side eye, my mouth full of breakfast. "Um, what?"

He'd placed one of my mother's speed dating card packs on the table, with one flipped over: *What's the meaning behind your name?*

"You stole a pack of cards from last night?"

"Oh, shit." Jet's face had turned ashen as if he had committed grand theft auto.

I grabbed his hand. "Wait." I swallowed the last bite of French toast, trying to ignore the zing of electricity up my arm from touching him. "It's okay. Keep them."

Jet inhaled through his nostrils, completely still.

"So, what kind of name is Jet?" I removed my hand and, after a beat, he laughed, a full belly laugh, wiping his eyes.

"It's short for Jethro." His cheeks pinked.

Something from my childhood watching reruns on regional TV stations came to mind. "Oh yeah, Jethro Cummings. Were you named after the Beverley Hillbillies character Jethro?"

"Ha, no. I'm named after Jethro Tull, the band."

I blinked with a shrug.

"They were kind of a big deal in the seventies and later. My parents were huge fans but had to settle for tribute band nights because Jethro Tull didn't tour Australia after their 1974 tour. They love to tease me that I was conceived during one of the tribute band concerts."

"Oh. My. God."

"I know, right?" His cheeks were pink again. He gave the speed dating card the stink eye. "These cards have some kind of voodoo. Not even sure why I said that."

"But it's true?"

"Yeah. I'm Jethro, and my younger brother is Tully."

"That's sort of sweet. It's a thing for some people to name people after where they were conceived."

Jet snorted. "Guess Jethro is better than 'pub's car park' or 'toilet stall at concert' or 'back seat of my dad's sedan'."

I snorted and then covered up by laughing.

Jet grinned. "Hey, it's not like I've ever asked where exactly at the tribute band concert they did the deed."

"So romantic," I said in a breathy voice, pretending to swoon.

The towel around my head unravelled, and I gave up on it, shaking out my shoulder-length hair.

"What about your name?" he asked, his voice deeper again. "What does Ari mean?"

"I looked this up once. Pretty random stuff." I found myself a little self-conscious. "It means lioness. Or 'of God'. It's Hebrew or something. Or it also can mean 'from a noble family'." I chuckled with a shrug. "Or it's sort of Welsh? It's formed from the Welsh word for silver. It's a versatile name across cultures and occasions."

I picked up my knife and fork and placed them on my plate.

"Silver lioness sounds badass," Jet murmured.

I huffed, not sure why I felt so pleased with the way he was looking at me or the way he said 'badass'.

"Nothing badass about me."

"I dunno, going on a solo trip around Australia by yourself is pretty badass."

"Mum thinks it's a dumb idea," I mumbled, my thumbnail tracing the grain of the wooden tabletop.

"Nah, definitely badass."

I looked up. Jet looked so sincere and genuine. He winked.

I looked back down at my plate. "Thanks. For breakfast and badassery comments."

"What's something your mother taught you growing up?"

Jet had chosen another speed dating card.

"Sorry," I whispered, feeling a cold lump in my stomach. "Hard pass on Debra." I chanced a peek at Jet as he stood, taking his plate. "What about you? What did you learn from your mother?"

"You really want to know?"

I nodded.

He put on the kettle and leant against the kitchen counter, studying me. The man looked at me like he could see my thoughts. I felt naked before him.

"You thought I was an idiot for believing in love, but I gotta admit, my parents are living proof it can happen. They are still in love, like teenagers. When I turned fourteen, Mum sat me down for a chat. She taught me never to go to bed angry with your partner, to treat women of all ages with respect and how to cook. Including French toast."

I smiled in spite of myself. Debra hadn't even taught me how to cook. Ash had done that.

"All I'm saying is you've only been with Wes, and on that basis, you've decided to give up on love."

My smile faded. "Dad left us when I was twelve, and I've never seen him since. He told Mum he loved her. He told me and Ash he loved us. He lied."

Jet's face fell. "I'm sorry." The kettle began its ear-piercing squeal. He flicked it off. "Look, I—"

"Still, that's only two men," I said, cutting him off while spearing more French toast. "Gotta be more examples out there of guys who mean it when they say they love you."

I bit into the French toast and groaned, my eyes rolling into the back of my head. *Divine.* I looked up to find Jet staring.

"Seriously," I said, holding up the last forkful of French toast. "This is sex on a plate. No, better than sex."

He coughed and cleared his throat. "Coffee?" He held up a French press.

"Heck, yes." I paused. "So I guess you know the whole story now about why I wanted rebound sex after Wes before I go on my trip."

"I'm sorry, Ari," he said again.

"What for?"

I didn't look him in the eye. I was distracted by the flex of his arm muscles as he pressed down on the plunger.

"This isn't pity, okay? I think you've had a shitty experience, and no one deserves that. On behalf of all men, I'm sorry."

I snorted, unable to stop my lips curling up.

Jet smiled back. "Milk? Sugar?"

"Just milk."

He smirked as he poured two cups of steaming hot coffee, adding milk in both and handing one to me.

"You sweet enough?"

"Ha. ha. Nah, just bitter."

He added two sugars to his mug with a wink. "I'm not."

A shot of heat went straight between my legs. I hastily stirred my coffee to avoid meeting his gaze.

My teaspoon fell into the sink with a clatter. "Want to go back to the van? Mum might appear at any moment, and I don't feel like dealing with her right now. Especially after her outright lie about being my sister."

For a second, I thought he'd say no. The van was cramped, too intimate, too messy.

"Sure," Jet agreed, his face neutral.

I headed straight to the back door and out into the yard, noting how dark the sky was. Another storm was rolling in. He caught me easily, slid the van door open and stood aside, waiting for me to go first.

"Why are you being so nice?" I blurted, flustered being so near him.

"Because I am nice." He frowned.

I was careful not to spill my coffee as I stepped up into the van. I sipped it, and oh yesss, he knew how to make a wonderfully strong, hot brew. Praise be to caffeine.

He *was* nice—more than nice—but what happened now? *Was he still expecting sex?* I groaned, not quite believing I'd thought that.

"I'll leave right after the coffee," Jet said. "Didn't mean to stay so long."

I looked up, and our eyes locked. A pang of sadness settled in my chest. *Why would I miss someone I barely knew? That's just absurd.*

One drop, then two, and then thousands of raindrops pelted down the van. We both looked at the van's pop-top roof as the rain came down in sheets and thunder crashed as lightning lit up the sky.

"Wait, you had a motorbike?"

"How'd you know that?"

"You had a helmet and your jacket."

We were both yelling to be heard over the storm.

"Bike's at the pub. Ryan said it should be safe locked up in the beer garden. I owe him for that."

"I have movies on my laptop if you wanna wait out the rain." I shrugged, trying to be casual. "With me. Here. If you want."

He stared over the rim of his coffee cup.

"I mean, it can't be good riding on a motorbike in this weather."

"True," he hedged. "What movies?"

"Some old school, some new." I shrugged again.

He grinned. "Way to sell it to me, Ari."

"Or, you know, be wet. Your choice."

Thunder boomed again, and lightning flashed, causing me to jump. Coffee splashed over the rim of my mug and onto my yoga pants.

"Storm wins." He passed a box of tissues to mop up the coffee. "You choose the movie."

I selected a recent Bond film and fell asleep soon after the opening scene, despite the coffee.

When I woke up, the sun was low in the sky, and I was under my duvet against something very warm and very hard. I stretched and opened my eyes to find myself looking into Jet's eyes.

"Comfortable?" he rasped.

I was. And was sprawled over him like a human blanket. "I fell asleep?"

"Yeah," he smirked. "You trapped me again."

"I think we both know you're not trapped."

"You underestimate your powers as the human blanket."

God, his voice was husky and rough. Up this close, I noticed just how full and kissable his lips were.

"Rain's stopped. I should go." Jet shifted, and I sat up with him but slipped and found myself straddling his lap. His hands flew to my hips to keep me from falling off the bed. The duvet fell to the floor.

We froze. Jet swallowed hard, his Adam's apple bobbing up and down. I fought an urge to lean in and lick it.

My head no longer ached from last night's wine. I felt so much better after my nap and his breakfast.

"How long was I asleep?"

"Three hours."

My knee started to slip on the sheet. Jet tightened his grip on my hips, and I gripped his biceps. "You're so strong."

"Shearer's muscles." His breath hitched. "Part of the job."

His arms twitched under my touch, his eyes glowing.

I leant in and pressed my lips against the corner of his mouth. His lips parted in surprise with a sharp intake of breath.

"Thank you," I whispered, pulling away.

"For French toast?" His voice was a hoarse whisper.

I smiled, shaking my head. "Being the man you said you were."

Slowly, we inched forward and kissed, tentative and slow. His tongue skated over mine, and I opened up to him, deepening the kiss. His hand slid up to my neck, his thumb cuffing my throat gently, and I moaned, pulling on his tee shirt. His grip tightened on my hips, pulling me against him. I saw stars as his erection grazed against my soaked underpants.

I swayed towards him when he pulled away. He blinked, released his hold on my neck and looked away. He was thoroughly dishevelled and bed-sexy with swollen lips, mussed dark brown hair, flushed cheeks and dark eyes.

"The storm's passed," he grunted.

I cupped his cheek, rough with a day's growth, and made him look at me. His head pressed ever so slightly into my touch.

"If I was doing your make-up on set, I would apply a liquid highlighter on your cheekbones here." I brushed the pad of my thumb across his cheek on the left and then right. "And then a little foundation, not too much, to match your skin tone. That's it. Your skin is just fantastic."

I let my fingers trace over his cheeks and chin and down his neck. He moaned, causing his whole body to tremble slightly.

"Must be the lanoline," Jet muttered, his voice rough. "In the wool. Sheep."

"Stay."

He stared for several seconds, and I stared back, surprised at how bold I'd been. My heart was racing.

"What do you want, Ari?" His chest rose and fell like his breathing was laboured.

"Will you stay and have sex with me?"

"You don't have to—"

"I *want* to."

He narrowed his eyes but didn't move.

"This isn't like last night. I want to, *with you*."

We watched my hand reach between us and slide over the zipper of his jeans to palm his obvious erection. I looked him in the eye, feeling a surge of confidence as he groaned, flexing his hips into my hand.

"But the question is, do you?"

5

Jet

Cupcake: What's your favourite colour?

I rolled my aching shoulders and eased back into my outdoor chair after throwing another small log into the metal drum acting as my bonfire-come-fire pit and clinked my beer against Blake's with a mutual 'cheers'.

"Can you believe Theo is dating Trixie?" Blake slumped into his seat. "About to shoot my shot with my all-time favourite country and western singer and he appears out of nowhere saying he's her boyfriend."

"I still can't believe Trixie is Tom Turner's sister."

Our eyes met and together we said, "Mind. Blown."

We each took a long drink of our beers.

I'd avoided the house—*my* house—for the time being, opting for a sunset beer with Blake in the backyard to celebrate the completion of the shearing at the Turner's place.

"Was a good contract at the Turner's," Blake mused. "I'd go back if they had me."

"Not just for a glimpse of Trixie?"

Blake grinned. "That's a bonus, of course. You know they still haven't found the shooter from her concert."

"Of course you know all the goss."

"Follow her on Instagram. Her morning yoga reels are —" He made a chef's kiss gesture and then sighed. "It's all happening here at Ballydoon. And you're staying in the thick of it."

"Yeah." Usually, we'd be planning where we would head for our next contract. But tonight, we were parting ways.

"First night here, hey?"

"Alone, yeah." I cleared my throat. "Where are you headed?"

"Armidale, and then Inverell if Armidale doesn't come good." Blake shifted his feet. "Theo asked me to be a mentor at shearing school for their next session."

I looked up. "He asked me, too."

We burst out laughing. "Sneaky bugger. Asking us separately."

"Knowing we'd talk about it with each other eventually."

We chuckled again, watching the sunset over the distant hills. Ballydoon and the Turner's homestead were just beyond that view.

"You going to do it?" Blake asked, his voice suspiciously casual.

"Maybe. Depends on this place. You are, aren't you?"

Blake nodded slowly. "Yeah, I am. Wouldn't mind giving it a go." He shifted in his seat. "Do you ever think about what would have happened to us if we hadn't gone to shearing school?"

"Oh yeah," I murmured. "I reckon we would have stolen cars until we were serving prison sentences. Or dead."

Simply named, "The Shearing School", the training initiative was run by the Department of Justice and New South Wales Police to give country kids a fresh start and work skills after a conviction as a juvenile.

And Blake and I, bored teens, drunk at fourteen years old after experimenting with the liquor in my parents' liquor cabinet, stole a car, took it for a joyride and crashed it into a fence.

The look on my parents' faces at the police station. The shame I had carried, and still did.

Theo was a former cop who volunteered at the shearing school and inspired us to get our shit together and stay out of trouble. And we had.

"Do you ever tell people about what we did?"

"Nah." Blake stretched. "Gotta leave that shit behind."

"True. But still, can't believe my grandfather left me his place, along with my brother."

"You're not fourteen anymore, mate."

"I know."

"Everyone does dumb shit when they are fourteen. We just did it all in one night and got caught."

The bonfire was low in the metal drum, and the dew was settling, bringing an icy chill.

"We should go inside. Hungry? Can cook up some snags."

"I miss Leonie Turner's cooking already. The spread at the Turner's was impressive." Blake put on a fake sniff and whimper. "Guess I'll suffer through your burnt sausages."

We downed our beers, and I let the bonfire burnt itself out, safe in the drum.

Finding cooking gear was a challenge. My grandfather just shoved anything anywhere into a cupboard at will.

"So, pouring beers," Blake said, finding a frypan in the Tupperware drawer. "You going to be happy with that?"

"I'm happy it pays my bills and puts food in my belly."

"Makes you wonder about that Ryan Turner."

"How so?"

"He's a bartender and also like Ryan Turner esquire running his historic sheep station in Ballydoon with thousands of livestock with his family, and yet he's pulling beers behind the bar. Bit like you now."

I avoided Blake's observation unnerving.

I had no idea why Ryan worked at the pub when he was also a mechanic and had to run his property.

"Not like my place is anything like the Turner's." I found cooking oil in with the coffee cups. "I will have to take everything out, clean it all and then organise the cupboards."

Blake chuckled. "Right on, Martha Stewart."

I was about to chip him for that comment but caught him staring at the counter where a fly was checking out breadcrumbs, then to the fruit bowl on the kitchen table.

Jesus, I had a fruit bowl now.

My life once fitted into motorbike panniers, and now I was the owner of an amber glass retro fruit bowl, dish drainers and welcome mats at the front door.

The Turners had fruit bowls and dish drainers and welcome mats.

My eyes pinged between the fly-humping stale breadcrumbs and the fruit bowl, unsure of what to do.

You idiot, shoo the fly, clean the bench, get the snags!

"Should've got you a housewarming present," Blake mused. "That's what you do, right?"

I quickly wiped down the countertop and the fly took off. "Honestly, I have no idea."

We both laughed as I threw the washcloth on the dish drainer. Blake's gaze strayed to the fridge where I had a magnetised calendar from a real estate agent, a shopping list scrawled in pen and a reminder to go to the hardware store in town.

I had lists now. And household maintenance.

"How do you do it?" Blake asked.

"Do what?"

"Just stay in one place?"

His gaze then strayed to the fruit bowl. Fruit bowls were for people who intended to stay in one place.

"Not sure, to tell the truth. I'll be able to tell you in a month or two. Feels weird not looking at the jobs boards or getting texts about shearing down south."

Our contractor would be texting us daily at the moment with work on various properties. Blake and I could afford to be selective too, knowing we were in demand with our good reputation.

Right on cue, Blake's phone pinged with a message. He glanced at the screen. "Huh. Looks like South Australia will need shearers earlier than thought this year." He pocketed his phone and looked around the room again. "But you're not coming, are you?"

I shook my head. "Think I'll make a go of it here. Besides, throwing drunks out of the pub is just like sending a cranky ram on its way down the chute."

Blake snorted, not looking me in the eye. "You know, seeing Theo again makes you think about what we were like back in the day."

"We were two little shits."

We both laughed. "That we were."

"And now?"

"We scrub up alright."

We laughed again, and I heated the frypan. "You're always welcome here, whenever you need."

Blake blinked fast. "Right. Thanks."

I caught how tight his jaw was, how his whole body was on edge. Blake had bounced around in foster care growing up and didn't speak to his parents. Now, he had no family home to go to.

"My sister's shacked up with a fella an hour away from here. Towards the coast in the hills. He sounds okay. They invited me for Christmas, and I'm going to pop in and, you know, make sure she's all good. That he's good enough for her."

Huh. Maybe her home would become a place he could always return to.

"Maybe I'll see you then or something."

"It's a date," I replied, stifling a grin and reaching for the snags.

"Speaking of dates, what happened at your speed dating night? You never said a thing."

I paused for a second, then two, and then let each sausage fall into the pan with a loud sizzle. "Nothing," I replied thickly. "Find some tongs, will you? These snags need to be flipped."

"WELCOME ABOARD." The pub owner, John, held out his hand, and I shook it.

Blake had left before I woke at six this morning, leaving a note 'good luck adulting with the house and shit'.

And now, eleven hours later, the adulting started with my first shift at the bar.

I'd pulled beers and served in a bar when I had turned eighteen and now found myself back at it at twenty-six.

Turned out that Ari's real sister, Ash, also used to work behind the bar with Ryan and was now working as a line order cook in the kitchen.

Ari. I inhaled a deep breath as my dick stirred at the memory of our night together a week ago.

Think of fencing wire, paint, strainer posts ... Money from bar work was essential to afford supplies for the farm and keep up my payments to buy my brother out. I had to start fixing fences to get it ready for half a dozen weaners I'd like to fatten up and sell before summer.

After spending the night with Ari, I'd retrieved my bike from where I'd left it at the pub to find several messages from Blake saying that extra hands were needed for the Turner's shearing clip. Several texts later, I met Ryan over a cup of tea with his mother, Leonie, and his younger brother Tom, on the veranda of their historic homestead at Ballydoon.

Thankfully, Ryan never asked or said a word about the speed dating night.

After the chat, Tom invited me to show my stuff in the shed. I took up the clippers in a stall and sheared a fine-looking merino ewe, taking her fleece off without a nick. I was offered the job on the spot.

Now, my bank account looked respectable after being paid for my shearing, but having a regular paycheck from the pub would help pay bills and keep food on the table in between scoring local shearing gigs.

In the storeroom behind the bar, I slipped off my leather jacket and missed the coat hook. As it crumpled to the floor, a couple of red and purple cards fell out of my pocket. *Debra's date night cards.* I smiled, stuffing them back into my jacket and, out of habit, opened my email app to check for new emails. One new one downloaded.

Congratulations! You've been matched!

Ariane Wilde indicated she'd like to be matched with you from the Ballydoon Single-Mingle night, and her contact details are included below. Your contact details have been forwarded to her as per your registration form.

Keep mingling and take a chance on love!

Debra Wilde

I grinned.

Holy shit, Ari. What a night we'd had in her van. She'd been incredible, fucking amazing. And I'd made good on my promise to her and made sure she'd orgasmed many times that night. Calling my name every time she came was the best thing I'd ever heard.

Shit. I adjusted myself. *Didn't need a boner in front of my new boss on my first day.* How my dick had any energy was beyond me. Since sleeping with Ari, I was rubbing one out every morning and in the shower at night.

We'd talked, too, long into the night and morning, about all sorts of things. But the next morning, she'd dropped me off at the pub to get my bike and then left. Just a goodbye, good luck and a thank you, and then she drove away in Bessie. No strings attached. No phone numbers swapped. No promises made.

By my calcs, she'd probably be at the Whitsundays, or even Cairns, by now, if she hadn't got distracted with other attractions along the way.

But now I had an email with her mobile number that she wanted me to have. I grinned and pulled out a card from my leather jacket.

I took a deep breath, copied the mobile number from the email, opened up my texting app and took a chance.

Ari

I PAID for the petrol and opened the maps app on my phone to compare it to the tourist paper map in my hand. I was checking out how far I was from the Airlie Beach caravan park when a text popped up, stopping me dead in my tracks.

> Unknown: Hi Ari, nice surprise to find you wanted to swap numbers *winky face*

> Unknown: So how's Bessie's muffler?

> Unknown: and what's your favourite colour?

I blinked at my phone's screen. If this was a scammer, this was a somewhat strange way of getting my attention.

> Unknown: Mine's Kawasaki green BTW. Just like my motorbike.

HOW RANDOM.

> Me: I think you have the wrong number.

> Unknown: Is this Ari?

WAIT A SECOND ... BESSIE, MUFFLERS, MOTORBIKES. MY THIGHS CLENCHED.

> Unknown: Got an email saying I was matched with you from the speed dating night.

Unknown: Keen to know how you and the van are going. I feel emotionally invested in Bessie

Me: Jet?

Unknown: Yep

Me: how did you get my mobile?!

Unknown: I told you we were matched. From speed dating.

I flicked back to my emails and tapped my foot as they downloaded. There it was. Mum had forwarded Jet's details with a brief message from the speed dating night that I had matched with him.

Bloody hell. *Mum!*

Unknown: Is everything okay?

Unknown: You sound freaked out, even for a text. I assumed you wanted to swap details? Cos of the email

I took a deep breath and swore.

Me: I think Mum took liberties and matched us.

Unknown: Ah. Shit. I'll delete your number. No harm done

Unknown: I never got to say I really enjoyed meeting you and our weekend together.

Jethro Cummings had delivered beyond his promise. I'd come four times. *Four!* With his tongue, with his fingers, and twice with, *ahem*, Wonder Dick.

He'd whispered affectionate nothings while we lay there, sated and boneless. *You're so fucking gorgeous ... You smell amazing, like honey and coconut.* My core tightened at the memory of how Jet's dirty talk had unravelled me every time. *I want the taste of your sweet pussy on my lips. Your tits are the best I've ever sucked. Are you ready to come so hard you'll forget your ex's name?*

Multiple orgasms were not an urban legend after all. Nor was I broken. Jet definitively proved that Wes lacked in sexual talent. Jet was a master between the sheets; he knew where to touch me and kissed me in places I didn't even know would turn me on. And he whispered, sweet-talked and outright commanded me in bed.

I fanned myself with the map.

It had been a week since I drove off, dropping him off at his motorbike, a Kawasaki model that was a bright lime green, at the pub, watching him in the rear-view mirror. Every night since, I'd thought about our one-night stand and had to deal with how turned-on I'd felt.

One night someone had yelled back to keep it down.

Pro-tip: climax softly in a crowded caravan park.

> Me: You don't have to delete my number

I saved his number, briefly considering adding him as 'Jet—Wonder Dick' but deleted the reference to his penis. Like I'd forget.

I tapped my foot, waiting for a reply. Maybe he wouldn't want to text.

> Jet: This isn't weird?

YES. Sort of? A little?

Me: No. Well, a little bit ... but I'd like to talk

Me: And I really enjoyed meeting you too

And the Understatement of the Year Award goes to Ariane Wilde.

Jet: *smiley face emoji*

Jet: So, Silver Lioness, enjoying your road trip so far?

Jet: And how's Bessie? Muffler holding up?

I paused, enjoying the jolt of pride that he'd remembered the meaning of my name.

But I hadn't felt like a lioness this week—more like a cowardly lion. I'd almost turned back several times to drive back home to hide in Ash's house to watch Netflix and comfort eat into oblivion. Somehow, I kept driving north and found myself in Airlie Beach with plans to get to Cairns in a week or two, and then a week or two after that, hook a left and head to Mt Isa and onto Darwin before the wet season closed the roads. Maybe see Kakadu and dinosaur museums on the way.

I clutched the old-school tourist road map and steadied my breathing.

Me: Bessie the van is a champion on the highway. Everyone waves to me. No problems with the muffler, thanks to you

Jet: So, what is your favourite colour, Ari?

I snorted.

Me: Why do you want to know that?

Jet: It's the first card I picked at random

Me: you still have my mother's speed dating cards?!

Jet: ha, yeah. Still had them stashed in my leather jacket. Just found them again

Me: fine, but we're not on a date or anything

My stomach gurgled again, and I rubbed it, feeling weird about that text. Of course we're not on a date. We're just texting.

Me: Not pink. Not girlie.

Jet: Okay. So what is your favourite not pink and not girlie colour?

Me: It's blue but a special kind of blue. It's the blue of the sky when the sun has just set at twilight. That blue is the best blue, and the best colour, in the world. Being in Sydney for four years, I loved the blue of the water at North Head and in the harbour, but coming home to Ballydoon, it's the blue of the sky on a cold night that's my favourite colour.

Jet: That's really beautiful

Jet: I don't think I've noticed the blue of the sky at twilight. I'm gonna check tonight

I sucked my lips to prevent a smile spreading across my face, feeling ridiculously pleased with his compliment.

Me: Is yours really Kawasaki green?

Jet: Haha how about second fave? My fave is boring. It's cream—not the food, but the colour of a fleece you've shorn off with no nicks on the animal and the fleece is just perfect and of the finest quality. That cream colour is just perfect when you've been slaving away for a long, hot day in the shearing shed

Me: that's strangely beautiful. Even if cream isn't really a colour *winky face emoji*

Jet: you're going to diss my moment here? *insert smiley face*

Jet: right now tho, gotta say amber is my fave colour because I'm about to pull beers at the pub and then crack open some cold ones when I get home.

Jet: I sheared for the Turner family for their winter clip. Ryan the bartender is my boss now at the pub

An image of Jet, sweat glistening arms and chest, came to me in a flash. I let out a slow breath.

Me: that's great tho. Lots of extra cash to get your place set up.

We hadn't just spent the afternoon and night having sex in my van. Jet told me more about travelling around Australia for shearing jobs and his plans to do up his grand-father's house over winter and buy some ewes in a couple of months.

When I told him about my road trip plans, he never dissuaded me; he just listened and supported my ideas.

Jet: Absolutely. Money from shifts at the pub keeps my bills paid.

> Me: You'll meet plenty of women working there too. You know, to find true love

The bubbles kept moving and disappearing. My stomach lurched. Maybe I needed more car snacks.

> Jet: the pub, farm work and shearing take up all my time. Think I'll leave off looking for true love right now.

I felt pleased reading his text. Which also left me feeling immediately unsettled.

> Jet: speaking of work … I'm working right now. Can't be texting on the job

> Me: gotta go too. Searching for a caravan park

> Jet: talk soon, Little Miss Wilde

I looked up from my phone and saw myself reflected in the service station's glass doors. I was grinning like an idiot.

6

Saved Texts between Ari and Jet, June to September

Ari: Check out this sunset *inserts five photos*

Ari: I'm in Cairns. Went to the Daintree yesterday. Gonna stay here a week. snorkelling on the reef later today

> Jet: I can't begin to say how jealous I am looking at these photos

> Jet: it was minus 7 degrees last night. Froze the water trough too *three photos attached*

> Jet: fucking cold LOL

Ari: OMG WHO CARES ABOUT WATER TROUGHS! YOU HAVE FLUFFY LAMBS AND THEY ARE CUTE AS HECK!

Jet: They are indeed. Here are more photos of my weaners LOL *five photos attached*

Ari: I demand a daily sheep photo!

Ari: and omg weaners?!

Jet: Don't confuse other wieners with weaners LOL

Ari: what now!

Jet: These lambs are now weaned from their mums hence called weaners. And your wish for a daily wiener pic is my command

Ari: this is the first time I've had weaners sent to my DMs LMAO Keep them coming!

Jet: Spicy question: Give me two truths and a lie, and I'll guess the lie.

Jet: not technically a question, but I'll allow it

Jet: Not technically very spicy either, but I'll still allow it *winky face emoji*

Jet: Here goes: I've listened to a romance book on my phone, I've skydived and I've moved seven times in one year.

Ari: FINALLY! Where have you been?! It's been three days!

Jet: I don't get great mobile reception on the farm

Jet: I get your messages when I'm shearing, driving or on shift at the pub.

Ari: you can't use your phone at your house?

Jet: Landline phone. Old school

Ari: but internet. Like how?

Jet: Modem died in a storm. Don't have cash to replace it yet. So I just save my data on my plan and when I'm at the pub, I download songs, videos, pay bills etc

Ari: and porn

Jet: ha. Ha.

Ari: Am I wrong tho?

Ari: Hello? Jet? It's been a full minute and no word

Ari: have you disappeared because you're embarrassed??

Ari: and of course you read the romance book! It's awesome! So truth.

Ari: Skydiving is the lie. You already told me how your folks moved around all the time for fruit picking when you were young.

Jet: Fuck. I have no secrets anymore with you, Ari.

Ari: so you're going to tell me what you're downloading?

Jet: let me have my secrets, woman!

Jet: Holy shit ... Ari. Did you send me a photo of your tits?

Ari: you like?

Ari: And it's my new bikini—not my tits! I was sunbaking without the straps done up!

Jet: Yes. I do.

Ari: how do you know they're mine? Might be a random photo I found online to save you data

Jet: I remember your tits, Ari. Very well. Recognised that tiny mole on your left boob. And the scar on your right. You're ticklish in that spot

Ari: You remember my boobs from that one time?!

Jet: more than once, Ari. And you know it. And your tits are spectacular

Ari: Thanks *smiley face emoji* Consider the photo a gift for those cold nights and you need inspo

Jet: did you actually just encourage me to masturbate to this photo?!

Ari: Or this photo. Whatever's good

Jet: did you just send a photo of Bessie?

Ari: I know you like the van. Like a lot

Jet: You're killing me. I gotta go. Break over.

Ari: morning

Ari: just saying hi

Jet: morning

Ari: is this weird that talking to you every day feels right?

Jet: not at all *insert smiley face*

Jet: did you hear there was a huge arrest of the guy who shot at Trixie/Lily Turner at the Turner's property? News crews from everywhere here. Trixie/Lily is okay.

Ari: caught the goss via the Gram and Ash. Everything is hectic after I leave

Ari: Tropical North Queensland is simply amazing. Can't believe this is winter *photo attached*

Jet: holy shit, that's a very … nice … photo

Ari: it's a cute bikini. Also saw a cassowary yesterday

Jet: that bikini will only make more weaners show up in your DMs *large eyes emoji*

Ari: ha. Ha. Ha. The only *wieners I allow in my DMs are your *weaners

Jet: look at you go, knowing your livestock from dic pics

Ari: bought a surfboard today. Going to learn to surf!

Ari: drat, turns out the Great Barrier Reef means all surf is completely ruined over here. Guess I'm hauling this across the country to learn somewhere else

Jet: Scored another shearing job just south of the farm. Small job, maybe three days. Might not have mobile reception

Ari: In Richmond for a couple of weeks. Am working at the pub—LOL LOL LOL! Sending postcard. This place is seriously cool. *three photos attached*

Ari: Some dino pics and a selfie of 'bar wench Ari'. I am seriously never doing this again. How do you do bar work?!

Jet: Drunks are surprisingly similar to stroppy sheep that don't want to get shorn. And then there's beer.

Jet: why don't you do make-up for work?

Ari: I don't really want to do that anymore. This road trip is about doing new things. I don't want to see another make-up brush or eyelash curler for the rest of my days!

Ari: this trip is about new things.

Jet: I reckon knowing what we don't want to do helps us figure out what we do want to do

Ari: would you be a farmer if it weren't for your grandfather leaving it to you and Tully in his will?

Jet: Probably not. I'd still be on the road for contract shearing. All I know is that it did happen and I'm giving it a go.

Jet: can say tho, I doubt I would have ever owned land and a house as a shearer.

Ari: try being a make-up artist in Sydney with Sydney real estate prices haha

Jet: haha, Bessie is better than Sydney real estate

Ari: I agree. shit, customers. Gotta go

Jet: what a week. Was a fire on the Turner property, followed by snow. Am thinking of joining Rural Fire Brigade.

Jet: The wombat at the Turner's place stepped on my foot and it's still bruised.

Jet: gotta go. Smoko is over. Talk later

Ari: You're getting beaten up by wombats?! Aren't you a strong shearer/farmer guy?!

Jet: wombats are armoured tanks of the bush, and I have a new level of respect for the buggers

Jet: Was doing more shearing at the Turner's this week and that MOFO wombat chased me. Wombats and me don't mix. I'll stick to sheep. Postcard finally arrived from Cairns. Now have four stuck above the bar. Punters love your adventures.

Ari: do you love getting my postcard adventures?

Ari: Can send more from Kakadu and Darwin and from dinosaur towns on the way to Mt Isa

Jet: Fuck yes. Keep them coming *smiley emoji*

Jet: my shift just started. Pub is pumping tonight. Turner family have a function in the beer garden. I'm on a quick break

Jet: did you go to school with Amanda Turner?

Jet: Enough time for a spicy question: what sexy scene from a movie turns you on?

Jet: No doubt from me: Jamie Lee Curtis in True Lies doing the strip tease for Arnie. When she lets go and gets into it, holy fuck, she's hot

Ari: Hey there shearer guy. I was in Amanda's year at school, and Stacey was in the grade below. Ash was in the same grade as her brother Tom and his twin sister Lily. Didn't know them very well.

Jet: so you're older than me

Ari: Am I now? how old are you?

Ari: Aren't you a little young for True Lies?

Jet: It's a classic!

Jet: I'm 26

Ari: Huh, I'm a cradle snatcher of the speed dating night. I should have asked you for ID LOL

Jet: only by a year … Come on Ari, what's your fave sexy scene?

Jet: sex dungeon scene from Fifty Shades or Mr Darcy wet shirt? lol

Ari: *laughing emoji* Neither. Although Wet Darcy is Hot Darcy

Ari: I don't have a favourite scene

Jet: you don't have a favourite scene that turns you on every time you see it?

Ari: I like to read sexy scenes. And listen to them.

Ari: I had to pull over Bessie the other day because the audio book I was listening to got hot real quick and the scene was *fire emoji*

Jet: I haven't read a book since they forced us to in high school

Ari: the books I read are NSFHS

Jet: NSFHS?

Ari: not safe for high school lol

Jet: soooo you read dirty books?

Ari: I do, shearer guy. With a guaranteed HEA every time

Jet: Got your postcards from Townsville and Charters Towers finally. Stuck them on the bar.

Jet: You know, we're like pen pals. You send me postcards

Ari: You send me texts. So pext pals

Jet: That's not a thing Ari …

Ari: it's totes a thing, Jet …

Jet: it sounds like sext pals

Ari: only if you don't know the alphabet.

Ari: you want to be my sext pal??

Jet: U serious?

Ari: *photo attached*

Jet: holy shit did you just send a nude?

Jet: Ari, this is your ankle *eye roll emoji*

Ari: if this was 1813, that was totally a scandalous text I just sent

Jet: you realise how ridiculous that sounds?

Ari: I stand by my comment. In the book I just finished—yes, the romance one—the hero is completely obsessed with the heroine's ankles. She keeps flouncing in her gowns and catches glimpses of them *fire emoji*

Jet: her ankles … what is with that?

Ari: not sure, but all he knows is he wants her. Wants her bad.

Jet: so if I'm your sext pal, do you want to know what I'd do to your ankles?

Ari: This had better not be some kind of weird sex kink …

Jet: I'd run a finger over your skin, kiss your ankle and keep heading up your leg, see where you're ticklish. And I already know you're ticklish behind your knees

Ari: that's it?

Jet: I'd keep going until you're begging me to be inside you. I'd hook both your ankles over my shoulders and fuck you and just before you're about to come, I'd kiss both and then finish you so hard you wouldn't even remember your name

Ari: holy shit

Jet: is that what you want as sext pals, Ari? Because the night with you in your van was hot. So if you want to send photos of your ankle, or any other part of your body, I'll be thinking about what it would be like to have my tongue, mouth, hands on every part of you, making you wet for me.

Jet: Ari?

Jet: Shit, I'm sorry. I read too much into your texts about sexting. Fuck, Ari. I thought you were flirting

Jet: Fuck, please. Talk to me.

Ari: I'm here.

Ari: Shit, Jet. I'm a little worked up here

Ari: I'll need to take care of myself now

Jet: You just

Jet: *large eyes emoji* Holy fuck. Like, touch yourself? Because of my texts?

Ari: you're *very good* at sexting

Jet: I'll never doubt the power of an ankle pic ever again.

Jet: Fuck. I am at full mast and I'm at work. And my break is almost up.

Ari: Think of that shearing job you have next week. Think of the south fence that fell over last week and how much it's costing you in repairs

Jet: Those were pretty good turnoffs but no offence ... just heard your mother outside the male toilets. That sorted out my problem

Ari: LOL! Debra to the rescue! Poor Wonder Dick! Now, if I was in town ...

Jet: Don't you fucking dare text another word

Jet: but if you're awake later ...

Jet: I will be late. Long shift at the pub

Jet: But I'm keen if you're keen

Ari: Text me when you're home and we can talk *winky face emoji*

❧

Ari

The first storm of spring was rumbling outside, bringing wind and rain. It was very late when my phone rang. Jet was calling, just as he promised.

We'd been texting for months now after our speed-dating hook-up. Lots of friendly banter. And calls. Mostly to watch movies together, both of us bored or killing time. Our banter had been flirty, but nothing has happened. I was guilty of pushing the line on just being friends so many times.

Those photos of me in my bikini were a thirst trap. And I'd totally sent them to him to see his reaction. And he'd been a gentleman, driving me crazy as well as managing to impress me.

But this call felt different, and it wasn't just the rolling thunder outside and lightning adding to the effect. It felt like things were shifting up a gear.

I hit 'accept'. "Hey." There was the sound of water in the background. "Hello?"

Someone cleared their throat. "Hey, Ari."

Jet. My belly fluttered a little. Of course it was, his name was right there. "What are you doing?"

"Having a bath."

My brain short-circuited. Jet was wet and naked and talking to me. "Grandad's old claw foot bath was begging to be used, and I wanted a beer. A beer bath outranks a shower beer every time because I don't have to fucking stand up."

"If you're tired—"

"I am more than fine to talk to you. Besides—" The water slapped the sides of the bath as Jet moved. "We need to talk about how you've been hinting for a while now you'd like to do more than just text and talk."

His voice was gruff and deep.

Did I dare change what we were and become sext pals?

This was casual thing between us. I was a thousand kilometres away. More like three thousand.

What were a few sexts every now and again?

"And you should know I've had more boners at work than I care to admit. So, Ari, we need to sort this out."

"Okay," I replied briskly. "Yes, we do."

Jet groaned, the soft slap of water against the sides of his bath in the background as he moved. "Ari, if you were serious, just give me permission."

He spoke so softly I thought I'd imagined it.

"For what?" I whispered back. "Why do you need me to permit you to do something?"

It felt like the whole caravan park was listening at my window right now. Everything was so still and quiet, and my whisper was echoing off the van walls.

"Because it's about you." His voice was a raspy growl.

"W-what do you mean?" I asked, hating my stammer.

"Like I said, Ari. Getting your flirty texts at work leaves me in a situation. And right now? I'm hard, Ari." I sucked my lips to stop a whimper from escaping. "And I want to touch myself thinking about you. But only if you let me."

Woah.

But also, asking permission meant he wouldn't if I said no?

"If I said no, you'd ... stop?"

In the midst of being extremely turned-on, I was also curious.

"Course," he snorted. "And then I would hang up and take a two-hour cold shower."

I was flustered. I needed a bath or a very long, cold shower. "You think about me?" I squeaked.

No man or boy had ever admitted they thought about me during self-care.

"Are you kidding?" Jet scoffed again, and water splashed again. "We talk or text every day."

"I meant, do you really think about me like that?"

Jet chuckled a lovely deep rumble. "Ari, we've fucked. My dick has a nickname as a result."

"I know." Oh, how I knew. Wonder Dick™ had well and truly earnt his nickname.

Another delicious rumble.

"I know you know."

"But, you really think about me like that since we just had one night together?"

There was silence, then the pop of his lips as he finished a sip of his beer.

God, those lips of his. They'd be wet from his beer, wet from the bath. I swallowed hard. Was I panting?

"I think about you and our night, and I also think about how you're now a friend." His swallow was loud enough that I could hear the action over the phone. His tone was sincere, nothing condescending or sarcastic.

"You're my friend, too. I can't imagine not talking to you or texting you."

"So, Ari, can I tell my friend how I feel right now?"

My heart rate spiked. "Y-yes."

Moving my legs sent a bolt of pleasure everywhere. Just not quite delivering what I needed. And all we were doing was talking about being friends.

Weren't we?

"I feel comfortable flirting with you and playing around with you and talking about anything you fucking want to."

"Me too."

"But I've never jerked off thinking about you because it didn't feel right. Felt skeevy. Like I was doing you a dirty."

And I realised I'd done the same, in a way. I'd thought about our night in the van, how good it had felt. How he'd dirty-talked. But it was all blurry when I did think about it. Hazy, sexy memories.

"So, Ari, I gotta know. Can I think of you while I touch myself?"

"Do you mean fantasise about me?"

"Oh yeah. I want you to be the star of the show in my head."

"Yes," I panted. "You can, if you want to."

Jet let out a low groan. There was a clink of his beer bottle on something hard. Tiles? And then more water splashing.

"Fuck, Ari."

Was he doing it right now? Was his hand wrapped around Wonder Dick, pleasuring himself while talking to me?

"And Ari?"

"Mmmm?" My head was spinning.

"You can too, if you want."

"C-can what?" My voice was a breathy whisper now.

He chuckled again and then groaned. "Touch yourself

thinking about me doing every dirty thing you can imagine to you. You're allowed, too."

I moaned and Jet grunted. "Babe. I ... I gotta go." He chuckled softly. "You know why."

"Night, Jet."

"Night, Ari."

7

Spicy question: What's the wildest thing you've ever done?

Bessie was a glorified paperweight and luggage locker.

I kicked the dust on the side of the road. No one was coming from the north or the south. Not even a grey nomad caravan was in sight. Or a road train. Or even a farmer in a ute.

Thirty minutes' drive south was the highway. Too far to walk.

I was stranded.

And thinking about the texts Jet and I had exchanged over the last week and how one photo of my ankle had escalated our online conversation quickly. As I drove between lava caves, dinosaur museums and homestead tours, the rainforest giving way to red dust and rocky gorges, we'd kept flirting; our messages now seemed charged. Electric.

Even since our call when he wanted permission to think

about me. That he'd denied himself thoughts about me when he was alone.

Until I'd said he could.

And I'd not calmed down since.

Until now, with Bessie cooling my libido after coming to a stop following a loud clunking sound.

Last night, Jet's shift had gone two hours over, thanks to a blocked toilet that needed attention, late-night beer deliveries and an overnight guest requiring an ambulance. He'd texted an apology for being so late getting home. I'd texted back this morning but hadn't heard from him when I'd left the campground to head to Mount Isa for the rodeo.

My first rodeo and yet, I wasn't feeling interested in finding a cowboy or watching the action. I was more interested in talking to a shearer who'd just started farming.

But right now, I was between Julia Creek and Somewhere Else, down a side road to a pretty gorge where I'd had a swim and took photos, and now had one bar of reception on my phone and less than ten percent battery, waiting for roadside assistance.

And feeling frustrated in more ways than one.

The operator had warned me it could be at least a three-hour wait when I'd lost signal and the call disconnected.

In three hours, I could daydream about sexy cowboys and bull riders. But I kept thinking about a shearer-now-turned-farmer who liked baths.

Ugh, Jet and I were just friends.

Friends who constantly flirted and who had a thing one night. Who knows how our phone call last night would have gone if he hadn't been held up with pub emergencies?

I sighed, knowing what I wished had happened last night.

I patted Bessie's side mirror. Three long hours. Poo Bessie.

I checked my phone. I had one bar of mobile reception again.

> Mum: when are you planning on coming home? I've still got your position open at the salon.

> Mum: let me know

> Mum: and send me a postcard. I'm your mother, Ari. I know you send postcards to that lovely Jet fellow. I've seen them at the pub. I deserve at least one!

I kicked at a rock and sent it flying. Meddling matchmaking Mother Dearest who also wanted to be my boss.

My phone beeped with three more incoming messages.

> Jet: hey Ari. Sorry again for last night. Just woke up and saw your texts

> Jet: Going to see Trixie B and the Hustlers at the pub tonight. As a customer, not working LOL

> Jet: Maybe we can talk after that, if it's not late

> Me: hey

> Jet: you okay? What's wrong?

How could he tell from a one-word text?

Before I could reply, my phone rang, and I accepted his call, praying to the Gods that low power mode didn't chew through my phone's battery.

"Hey, Jet," I said, mustering as much enthusiasm as I could.

"What's wrong?"

"Why would anything be wrong?"

"Ari, you don't just text 'hey' when things are okay."

"Well, actually. I'm just feeling a little lonely. Bessie broke down and—"

"Bessie is broken?"

"Something in the engine made a loud noise, and Bessie just stopped. Roadside assistance is on the way, but I have a bit of a wait. And very little phone battery."

"Fuck, Ari. Are you going to be okay? How long a wait?"

A ute appeared on the horizon. "Oh, someone's coming!"

I pulled one headphone out, keeping Jet on the call as the ute pulled over. Five young men about my age were crammed into a dual cab ute with an impressive bull bar, floodlights and several antennas. Three pig dogs were leashed on the back tray, wearing metal and leather plates over their chests, their pink tongues hanging out, looking very happy.

I blinked, keeping my smile fixed, staring.

The dogs really were wearing breastplate armour.

"You alright?" said the driver, grinning, with a nod to Bessie.

"Van broke down."

They all looked at Bessie and then back at me. One crunched the can he'd finished drinking, tossing it to the floor.

"Ari, what the fuck is going on?" Jet rumbled through my headphone. "Is that roadside assistance?"

"Are you hunting pigs?" I asked, sending Jet into over-load with questions in one ear.

"Yeah, that's the plan. You called roadside assistance?"

"Yeah, I did, but it's a long wait. Three hours."

"That would be right." They all chuckled. "Cos I'm one

half of roadside assistance, and this is my day off. Jump up in the front, love. We'll give ya a lift to town. Name's Macca, by the way."

His mate in the front passenger seat jumped out and hauled himself up onto the back tray, giving each of the dogs a pat.

"Oh, I'm Ari. And thank you!"

Jet's gravelly voice filled my left ear through my headphones. "Don't get in the ute with strangers, Ari!"

"This is great! Let me get my things," I said to Macca and then turned to Bessie to retrieve my tote and backpack. "Hush, it's fine," I whispered into my headphone mic.

"You've told them roadside assistance is hours away and that you're alone and now they know your van too!"

"This isn't *Wolf Creek*, Jet!" I gritted out.

"How do you even know he's roadside assistance?" Jet demanded as I turned back with a plastered smile.

Macca looked at me like I was certifiably insane. "Are you on the phone?"

"Yes, to a friend." I sighed. "He doesn't want me to go with you."

"Get his licence plate and give it to me!" Jet yelled.

I winced. "He wants me to send your licence plate details to him."

Macca shrugged. "All good. I'd do the same if you were my missus."

I rattled off the numbers and letters to Jet. "I'm going now. I'll be fine."

"Text me, call me. I'm not happy about this, Ari."

"I can tell," I grumbled. "Of course I'll let you know. I'll be fine. Goodbye."

I hung up and got into the ute. The guys in the back were drinking rum. They all gave me big, cheesy grins. I didn't even want to think about how they were drinking before shooting at wild pigs.

The dogs barked excitedly, and the lone guy on the tray held on with the lazy confidence of someone who'd done this many times before.

"Lucky we found ya, 'ey?" Macca said, revving the engine and pulling out onto the road.

I smiled nervously and gripped my phone. "Absolutely. Lucky me!"

~

Jet

FIVE HOURS LATER, Ari finally called.

"Ari! Where—"

"Bessie is tucked in for the night at a petrol station that has a mechanic, and we are both safe."

"You don't just get in a car with strangers, pig dogs and guns!"

"But Macca was the roadside assistance, and he showed me his ID in the ute when we drove off, and it was his rostered day off, but he and his friends weren't going to leave me by the highway. And yes, they had guns, but they had them locked up and not loaded, and they are hunters in their spare time, and they take their dogs to properties to hunt for pigs."

"What the actual hell, Ari?" I blurted, breathing hard.

"The driver. Like I said, one of two roadside assistance chaps in town." Ari hummed with excitement. "And he's getting married in five days. And Davo, he was sitting in the back, he's having relationship trouble with his missus, hence the rums they were drinking, and the rest of them were sweeties, really."

"Rum? They were drink driving?"

"No! Macca was sober as a pig dog. Anyway, Davo isn't a hunter and was along for the ride to moan about his woman troubles."

I was going to burst a blood vessel. "Where the hell are you right now?"

"Cloncurry, in a motel. Macca and his friends are going to the rodeo too and are giving me a lift."

"Five random blokes drinking rum who own firearms are taking you to a rodeo." My heart rate was hammering away. Was this how you got a stroke?

"Jet, I was fine! They're nice. Besides, did anything come from his licence plate?"

"It was a registered vehicle."

"And?" Ari said in a sing-song voice.

"I also rang the local police station, and they confirmed he was roadside assistance." I sighed. "And they said he was getting married in five days."

"I know you did. Met the officer. Good mates with Macca. I'm sorry I worried you. It's nice to know you've got my back."

"We're friends, Ari. That's what we do."

There was a knock in the background at Ari's end.

"Hang on, someone's just at the door."

I pressed my phone against my ear on maximum volume to snoop on what was happening.

"G'day," a woman said. "Heard ya got picked up by Macca today."

"News travels way fast round here," Ari answered. "And I'm guessing from your red hair, you're his bride-to-be, Kayla. Congratulations!"

"Ha, yeah. His buck's night with the boys was going to be tomorrow at the rodeo."

The rodeo trip was actually a buck's night?! *Oh, hell no!*

Kayla continued before Ari could answer. "Look, Macca said ya did make-up for TV? Any chance ya could do my wedding make-up? The beauty chick has up and cancelled on me."

"Oh, umm ..."

"Be nice to have make-up done proper, you know? Look swish in the photos and that. Pay ya cash."

"Well ... um."

Kayla said an amount and Ari agreed, and then a door closed, presumably with Kayla leaving.

"I just got a job. Bridal make-up," Ari said in a rush. "Macca told his fiancé I'm a make-up artist."

"Yeah, I heard." She really had told Macca a lot of her personal details during the drive to town. "Surprised you accepted."

Ari inhaled sharply. "What does that mean?"

"Nothing. It's just ..."

"What?

"You said last week you didn't want to do make-up stuff anymore."

"Yeah, well, it's not like TV make-up. Been a while since I've done bridal make-up. And it's a cash job, and I have a cracked piston and towing costs to pay."

I remained silent.

"I need the money," Ari insisted and moaned. "Jet, am I weird for not wanting to do make-up anymore?"

"I don't know anything about make-up, Ari." He chuckled.

"Like, I mean ... am I weird that I want to do something completely different? It's not a Wes thing, although that's a part of it. It's just ... I was good at make-up but I've never really cared about it, and I want to do something I care about."

"Not weird at all. That sounds awesome."

"The thought of doing make-up professionally makes my stomach twist. I guess it's to do with Wes but ... also, I genuinely want to do something else with my life." There were muffled noises, like Ari was getting settled. "Do you care about sheep?"

He chuckled softly. "I care about not cutting them. I care about doing a good job. I guess I'm discovering what it means to look after them. I know nothing about looking after livestock. Never even had a pet."

Ari gasped. "This is a travesty. One that should be rectified."

"One thing at a time." I paused, knowing exactly her panic, the fear of being on the edge of stopping one thing and trying to find another living. "Tom Turner's been really helpful with my questions. He's given me good ideas for my place. Said he's happy to mentor me."

I swallowed at a lump in my throat. "So I get it, what you're trying to do. And there's nothing wrong with doing make-up for money while you are figuring it out. Scored some shearing contracts locally for a couple of small land-holders. The money will come in handy."

"That's so great, Jet." Ari sighed. "I just wish I knew what I wanted to do."

"Keep on searching. Don't let a cracked piston stop you from figuring out who you are."

"Or pig hunters?" Ari chuckled.

"Ha. Ha." I paced about in my living room. "I have to tell you something."

"Okay. Spill the tea."

"Something from my past. I may have overreacted about your break down because of dumb decisions I made when I was fourteen. I stole a car with a mate. I was drunk on cheap scotch we'd nicked from Blake's foster dad. We were bored, listless, and thought we were bulletproof.

"Had no money, no friends. No Nintendos or whatever. Not even a bike. Or a phone. Let alone a laptop. I already knew how to drive from learning off Pop in his paddocks in his rusty ute. Mum and Dad were away for work, so one night, me and Blake stole a car. Took it for a joyride and we crashed into a fence post.

"I was sentenced to an experimental farm for youth in the justice system. Nothing dodgy; it was a shearing school. I learnt to shear, and it probably saved my life."

Ari said nothing.

"I'm a shearer because I totalled a car under the influence and put not only my life at risk but also my friend's and everyone else on the road, and I totally understand if you don't want to talk to me again."

"Why would I do that?" Ari blurted. "God, Jet. I'm sorry I was casual about getting a lift."

I shrugged, even if she couldn't see me. "Some people have shunned me because of that dumb stunt when I was young."

"Well, I'm not. I won't," Ari whispered. "So, um, are any of your tattoos prison tatts?"

I burst out laughing.

"What?" she growled.

"First of all, I was fourteen, so nobody was inking up a scrawny teen. Second, I never got arrested again after that fiasco with the car. Never been to prison." I spluttered another laugh. "Are you disappointed I don't have prison tatts?"

Ari made a whiny noise.

"Why, Miss Wilde, did we just unlock a kink?"

She made the noise again and just maybe a kink had unlocked. Huh.

"I loved *Prison Break* at the time. Wait a second, is that why you can't believe you have now inherited your grandfather's place?"

My head spun at the abrupt change in conversation. "Maybe, a little?" A whole damn lot and you know it. "Have you ever owned a place? Or had a mortgage? You know what I mean?"

"Mum's always rented. And so have I in Sydney." Ari laughed. "Closest thing I've come to home ownership is the van. Probably will be for my entire life, too."

I laughed with her. "I had an old Toyota HiAce, and I mean old. It leaked when it rained, thanks to rust. But it was home on wheels for a few years getting to shearing jobs. Then I got my bike and stayed in shearers' quarters or slept in my swag. Until now."

"Are you okay about inheriting your grandfather's place?"

"Yeah?" Panic slithered through my chest, hot and slippery. "It's just a lot to take in. Never thought this would happen."

"But it has."

"Yeah. Still smells like Pop, you know?"

Ari laughed softly. "That smell that grandparents have."

"Yeah, like talcum powder and soap or something." I inhaled a deep breath and smiled. "Like a hug. Like Christmas."

Ari sighed. "Did you have happy memories at your pop's house?"

"Yeah, as a kid. Christmas day here. Cold ham, always

prawns, salad. Swim in the creek if there was water. Presents, of course." I paused and then blurted, "I've invited my folks and brother to have Christmas at the house."

"That sounds really nice, Jet." A comfortable silence settled between us before Ari added, "Were you worried I'd not talk to you because of some dumb thing you did when you were fourteen?"

"A little?"

"I think a lot."

"Yeah."

"Well, don't be, Jethro Cummings. I think we have a lot more to talk about. Do you want to watch a movie with me?"

"I liked watching that Bond movie with you in the van."

"Ha, I didn't do much watching."

"How does this work? Watching a movie while you're in Cloncurry and I'm here."

"We find the same movie across all our streaming options and hit play at the same time. Oh, I've got *Star Wars*."

I found *Star Wars: Episode V* on a streaming service while Ari bought takeaway, thanks to the new modem. Sprawled on my grandfather's old couch, we watched the movie together. Ari went off about the Han and Leah's 'I love you, I know' exchange, and we settled in for *Episode IV*, texting back and forth what our Ewok names would be, with both of us falling asleep before the end.

8

Ari
Spicy question: How do you like to flirt?

"Hey, it's me."

"Oh, hey, you." Jet's voice was deep, sleepy, all sex and twisted sheets.

"Did I wake you?" *Oh God, had I interrupted him with someone else?*

"No, babe. I just … had my eyes closed while I had a bath."

Warmth diffused throughout my body at hearing Jet call me 'babe', especially when he didn't realise he did it, usually when he was exhausted.

"Big day?"

"Yeah, sheared some alpacas. They were a little feisty."

A ute full of guys drove past. Some of them yelled at me, and one threw a rum can over my head.

"Ari, what's wrong? What's going on?" Water splashed as Jet continued. "Are you okay?"

"I'm fine. Totally fine. I went to the rodeo and small world; I saw Emma Woodhouse from Stanmore here."

"Who's Emma?" Jet asked, his voice husky.

"Stanmore's reigning rodeo queen. I'm just walking back to Bessie, and I wanted to call you while I did."

"Who was that? What happened to Macca and friends?"

"You just heard some idiots leaving the rodeo. Macca and his mates are kicking on at a pub for his buck's night, and I wanted to get to bed."

"Are you safe?" he demanded.

I glanced around. I was safe, I guessed. But for some reason, I just wanted Jet on the phone. "Yeah, just feeling alone."

"Aww, you miss me."

"To be fair, I never knew you in Ballydoon. I know you as a text message and a phone call."

"True. And don't forget one night in your van."

I said nothing, allowing myself to remember the highlights of that night.

"If you'd stayed in Ballydoon," Jet asked with a groan, the water slapping the sides of his bath in the background. "Would you have gone out on a proper date with me?"

I snorted. "What? And miss out on being asked stolen speed dating questions?"

He chuckled. "Maybe. But you didn't answer my question."

"I don't know. I wasn't up for dating then."

"And now?"

I shook my head. "Now? Right now I'm lost and more than two thousand kilometres away from you."

"Fine, here's another question." He sighed into the

phone. I remembered how his breath felt on my skin as he panted towards his climax.

"Okay," I whispered. "Ask away."

"Where do you like to be kissed, other than on the lips?"

I coughed and picked up my pace, recognising a corner shop up ahead. The caravan park was another two streets from here.

"That's one of Mum's speed dating questions?"

"Yep, found it a week ago. Been saving this one up."

I was very aware that Jet was naked on the other end of the phone. Sure, he was having a bath, but that made it worse: he was wet and naked.

"You evading the question, Ari?"

"No," I said quickly as I turned the corner. I could see the big willow tree I'd parked under in the caravan park in the distance. "I'm just thinking."

"Want to hear my answer?"

"Yes."

"Well, Miss Wilde, it's not the place you're thinking, although I do like attention down there." He chuckled, and I heard the *pfft* of a bottle top. "Bath beer. Been saving this up for tonight. So, I like to be kissed at the top of my leg, the bit which isn't your hip, drives me insane. It's ..." His voice trailed off in thought. "I'm staring at it right now. Hard to explain."

"Take a photo," I breathed, fumbling my van keys in the dark.

"You want me to take a photo of myself naked in the bath?"

"Yes."

I yanked the door across and leapt inside. Ever since I sent him the photo of my ankle, we'd flirted. Lately, our texts had been more and more explicit and suggestive.

I slid the van door closed with a thud and locked it. "I'm in the van, safe."

"Very glad to hear that." There was shuffling and water splashing. "One moment."

"Jet?"

Glass clinked on tiles as more water splashed. "Okay, you should get a photo soon."

My phone pinged on cue. My hands trembled as I switched to speaker phone and opened my texts.

Jet had only texted one word: *here*. A photo was attached.

I clicked on it and inhaled sharply. It was a close-up, but I could tell Jet had stood up in the bath, soap suds trailing down his skin and taken a photo with him pointing to his V-shaped muscles above his right leg. *The groin?* I had no idea what they were called.

Heck, he could call them Henry or George for all I cared.

Fucking delicious is what I was calling them from now on.

Beads of water clung to his skin, and now I understood what was meant by being thirsty. There was nothing more I'd like to do but run my tongue up that muscle group.

His finger pointed to the soft skin at his pelvis.

I wanted to kiss him there right now.

An ache pulsed between my legs.

"And no, it's not Wonder Dick."

"Ha. Ha."

"Like what you see?" Jet asked, his voice dipping an octave lower.

"Yes."

"I can tell by the way you're moaning." He chuckled again. "Are you turned on, Ariane?"

I bit my lip. He used my full name, and I was staring at his naked body. "Yes," I breathed.

"Fuck." Jet swallowed hard. "And where do you like to be kissed, other than on the lips?"

I shuddered. "Lots of places."

"I remember a few."

"I wish you were here right now."

"Why, Ari?" Jet moved in the bath. "I want to hear you say it."

"So you could fuck me."

He groaned. "Ari ..."

"Phone sex," I blurted, settling back on the bed.

Jet cleared his throat. "Like, have sex over the phone, right?"

"Yes."

"If you're still wearing clothes, they need to go, Ari. I'm a few steps ahead here."

"Are you hard?"

"As fucking steel, babe. Hurry."

I pulled my shirt off and tugged my jeans down. "Can I watch you?"

There was a splash and Jet swore.

"Jet?"

"Fucking dropped my beer in the bath," he muttered. Glass clinked on the tiles again. "Are you serious, Ari? You want to watch me jerk off?"

"Oh, yes."

"Do I get to watch you?"

"Fuck, yes."

My bra finally snapped open, and I wriggled out of it. "I'm undressed, except for my undies."

"Fuck." He groaned again. "I need to see you. I'll call on video."

The phone went dead, and in that moment, my body flushed with heat that we were finally doing this; then, I panicked about how I was going to do this using my phone.

My mobile rang. I hastily shoved it on the kitchen bench, propped it against half a loaf of bread and hit accept.

Jet's face filled the screen. "Ari ... holy fuck, you're naked." He scrubbed his face, groaning. "You're fucking gorgeous, Ari."

"I can't see you," I whimpered.

He placed his phone on what I think was his bed and then his hand covered the screen.

"Are you okay?" I asked as something dropped to the floor, then muffled grunts.

Suddenly, he was there: naked, still wet from his bath, on his knees. His cock jutted up towards the ceiling, the vein underneath pronounced.

"Like the view?" he smirked and began slowly stroking his length while he rolled his balls in the other, tugging slightly.

I'd never got to kiss or suck him the night we'd slept together. Oral wasn't something I'd been into until now. My whole body ached to be with him right in this moment. Where was teleportation or warp drive when I needed it, so I could be there to push him back onto the bed and take him into my mouth, his balls in my hand and make him come down my throat?

"Jesus, Ari. I like that idea too," he growled.

"Huh?" I blinked.

"You were muttering away under your breath what you'd like to do to me. Guess you like watching me like this?"

I looked into the camera lens and nodded. "I want to touch myself."

"Do it."

I slipped my hand between my legs as he released his

balls and braced his arm on the headboard, not pausing his strokes of his cock; slowly up and then slamming down to his root.

"Open your legs, babe. I need to see you."

His voice was so commanding, rough. I did what he said. My knees fell open, exposing myself to him on camera. My breath hitched, and I swirled my fingers around my clit, so hard and wet now.

"Fuck, oh fuck." Jet picked up his pace. "You're so fucking sexy, Ari."

I moaned and slipped one finger inside. Jet responded with a grunt. "Now two, babe. And faster."

I did as I was told. With my other hand, I squeezed my right breast, letting my fingers roll my hard nipple and then my left.

"Fuck yes."

My body shuddered, my head rolled to one side and then to the other, the sensation almost overwhelming.

"I want to see you come!" I cried. "Jet, I'm so close."

I watched him thrust into his grip as he growled.

"Now, three fingers. I want you to feel what my cock would be like inside you right now."

I gasped as I did so.

Jet let go of the headboard and gripped his length with two hands. I increased my pace to match the rhythm of his hips.

"Tell me how it feels."

"So good," I moaned. "Not as good as Wonder Dick."

He barked a laugh. "Fuck, Ari. I'm about to explode. Are you with me?"

I whimpered, my thumb rubbing against my clit every time I pumped my hand. His eyes were fixed on my hands, my pussy.

"I'm imagining you on your knees, begging for me to fill you and make you come."

I cried out as the first tremor took me by surprise. On my phone's screen, we locked eyes. "Oh God, yes!" I hissed.

Jet panted as he slammed his curled fists around his cock, his eyes fixed on me. "Fuck, *fuck!*"

I called out his name, my back arching off the bed as my orgasm seized my whole body in waves of pleasure. I forced my eyes open, eager to watch him find his release.

Watching him come was the most erotic thing I'd ever seen. I kept up the pressure on my clit, panting his name as he rolled his hips with an unrelenting pace into his fisted hands, my name on his lips. He threw back his head with a cry, sweat running down his neck and his chest, and he came. One thrust, two, three and four.

More tremors shook me as I watched.

He gulped for air as he came one last time into his hand and fell forward, bracing himself again on the headboard with one hand. With his cum on his hands, his chest and his arms, he was beautiful. Muscles twitched in his back, ribs, biceps. He was spent, wrecked, sated: all because of me.

An aftershock of pleasure rattled me at the fantasy of Jet coming on me.

"You okay, babe?" he sighed.

I took my hand away and hugged my stomach, floating on air. "Could only be better if you were here."

"Babe," he breathed. "I just ... need to clean up."

I grinned and nodded.

"Don't go away. I'll be right back."

I lay in the van, boneless.

Jet returned, still shirtless, with a lazy grin on his face. "So, tell me about your day."

I giggled. "Having my work with kids permit from my

film and TV work has come in handy. I did face painting for a daycare centre. Caravan park owners' daughter works at the centre, and we got talking when I checked in, and I mentioned my previous work. Boom! Cash job. And I have Macca and Kayla's wedding to do. So nice there's a bit of cash coming in. Might do a tour or two when I reach Darwin."

"Nice one, Ari." Jet kept on grinning, and I smiled back.

"And what about your day?"

"I've fully fenced the largest paddock now. Am thinking I'll get more sheep at the next sales. If I have enough cash. Tom's advice has been invaluable. I dunno how he knows so much stuff about sheep and farming." He closed his eyes with a sigh and then opened them again. "Sometimes I wonder if this is a mistake."

"I think you're doing great. Of course there's so much to learn. But you're not starting from zero. You're remembering what you do know from time with your grandfather."

"Sometimes I feel like a fraud. But then there's Ryan behind the bar with me, and he and his family are like a farming dynasty."

"If you want to stop, you can sell and do something else. You always have that choice."

"I know." Jet closed his eyes again. "I just want to make it work if I can."

"Yeah." My eyelids were heavy.

The last thing I remember was the rise and fall of his chest before I woke with a start to find myself in bed with my phone. The call had ended, but I had a message.

> Jet: you fell asleep. Wishing you a good morning when you read this later.

Jet: bonus question: Sweet or Spicy: what's your perfect way to spend a Sunday morning?

I smiled, realising it was Sunday morning. I allowed myself to daydream about waking up beside him, Jet saying good morning with a lazy grin, his hand sliding up my back, and falling back into bed, under him, on top of him, slowly building the pleasure between us to boiling point.

Me: sleeping in, feeling exactly like this

9

Ari

Goes both ways: What pick-up line made you laugh or melt?

Despite my fears, doing the bridal make-up for Kayla's wedding went very well. And led to a wedding invitation which led to my next job: kids' face painting. Someone had a sister in the next town whose kid was having a birthday party and desperately wanted a face painter.

The day after Macca and Kayla's wedding, I drove in a repaired Bessie to paint eight kids' faces at a party and loved it. I played games with them and sang songs while they waited their turns. No one wanted contoured cheekbones: it was all about maximum glitter and rainbows. I even got a tip for my work.

Jet had mentioned he used to look at social media community groups for small shearing jobs between major contracts and would post that he was available for hobby farmers who needed small flocks shorn. I decided to give it a go and posted my availability for bridal or special night make-up or face-painting parties. I'd scored three more jobs and arrived in Darwin, feeling on top of the world and with cash in my pocket.

I breathed in the humid, salty air, spices and herbs from the food trucks and let the noise of the Mindil Beach Markets surround me. The last week in Darwin had been fun, if not a little weird. I was judging the place as where Mum had taken off as soon as I'd finished high school and left for Sydney. She'd been trying for years to get me to join her in Darwin, she doing hair and me doing nails and make-up in her salon. I'd never visited while she lived there, citing I was too busy between working on set and doing TV station work, as well as the end-of-year social season for Sydney's A-listers. Every socialite needed to be seen and photographed with A-grade contoured cheekbones and smoky eyes at Christmas parties.

But the glamour and demand of party make-up was now replaced by cloying humidity, palm trees and warnings to not swim at the beach because of crocodiles.

So far, the monsoon season had been underwhelming. But according to many in the caravan park, conditions could change in a matter of days or even hours.

And it was stinking hot and humid. Beachside markets at dusk, with the breeze coming off the water, was the perfect place to cool off.

A customer picked up a shell at a stall across from me, and the stallholder smiled. "Found that washed up on the beach at the next bay. Pretty, hey?" the stallholder said to the customer.

The shell was conical with spots on one side and a blush of pink at its opening, the same colour as the sunsets here at Mindil Beach. It was beautiful.

Jet's number lit up my mobile. He was calling earlier than I'd expected, even with the difference in time zones. My toes curled, gripping my sandals, recalling our last video chat. Him naked, pleasuring himself.

I was hot and cold all at once.

"Why hello there, Mr Cummings," I murmured.

There was a muffled argument on the other end and then a stranger spoke.

"Blake, hold him back. I'll see who he's drunk dialling. Um, hello?"

Just then, in the background, Jet shouted at someone to give his phone back.

"Who is this? I'm Tom, Jethro's friend." Cheers went up in the background. "Ah, Jet's drunk and banned from using his phone. What?" More muffled conversation, and then, "Bloody hell, he says he wants more pics of your hot ... ankles?"

I giggled. "That sounds exactly like Jethro."

"I love you, Ari!" Jet yelled into the phone and Tom laughed.

I squawked, unable to speak. The stallholder cast a glance my way, and I managed a tight smile.

"Blake, I said to hold him!" The background noise was now much quieter. "Ah, shit. He's really happy. And drunk. Very drunk," Tom added nervously. "Wait, Ari? As in Ariane Wilde?"

"That's me. Wait, Tom Turner? Amanda's brother?"

I knew Tom was mentoring Jet to improve his farm, but I didn't feel I could reveal how much I knew about them.

"Ha, yeah. Thought you were in Sydney."

"I got out. Was in town briefly, and then I hit the road."

"Wait a second, you're sending him postcards for the bar?"

"I do. I believe I have a following in the public bar. Bally-doon famous at last."

"Wait a sec, here comes trouble."

There was a struggle and the phone distorted.

"Give me my phone so I can talk to my girlfriend!" Jet yelled in the background.

I spluttered a laugh.

"Get away, you idiot!" Tom laughed. "Seriously, Ari. Is he giving you trouble? He's had a few too many for his birthday."

"His birthday?" Jet hadn't mentioned his birthday was coming up, or even today. "He didn't tell me."

The phone distorted again and then erupted into noise.

"IT'S MY BIRTHDAAAYYY!" Jet screamed.

"Oh my God." I grinned. "I'm going to send you a present, birthday boy."

"I've got a present for you, baby. Right between my—hey!"

"Christ! Get your hand off your crotch," Tom commanded. "Sorry, Ari. No, no! She does not need your drunken idea of a present. Shit, now he's sulking. So, you're his girlfriend?"

"No!" Adrenaline spiked through my body. "I mean, we're friends. And I'm a girl. With hot ankles. Ha!"

I laughed again, high pitched and strained.

Jet had started singing which seemed enough to distract Tom from my rambling panic.

"He's drunk. He won't remember being such a pain in the arse in the morning."

"Ari's so hot!" Jet shouted in the background. "I really like her. She's so smart ... and pretty. In a bikini."

Tom chuckled. "Sorry about this."

"It's okay," I replied, not taking my eyes off the shell as the customer turned it over, considering it.

"He wants his phone back. You sure you're cool with him in his current state?"

The customer put the shell down, and I pounced.

"Yeah, absolutely. Jet's … great. He's fine."

I held the shell to my ear, listening to the echo of the sea.

"Hey, babe. Sorry, I'm sorry about your ankles. And grabbing my dick. Wish you were here right now. That would be the best birthday present ever."

"So you've caught up to me then. I still wish I knew so I could have sent you a card or a present."

"I didn't … I just …" He happy-sighed, adding in a loud whisper, "Talking to you is the best present."

"I'll send you the ocean for your birthday."

He hiccupped. "Well … fuck. That's cool, too. But I dunno where I can put the ocean at my place."

I giggled. "And Jet?"

"Yeah?"

His friends were singing 'Happy Birthday' in the background, and suddenly I felt bold. "I like you, too."

"You do?"

"Yeah." My stomach fluttered. *He's just drunk. We're friends who flirt.*

"Hey, Ari, I'm looking at the moon right now. Can you see it, too?"

I looked up at the sky, and there it was, the moon rising over the pop-up stalls. "Yeah, I am. It's beautiful."

"I look at the moon every night, thinking about you, wondering where you can see it." Someone said something in the background. "Ugh, Tom says I gotta go, babe."

"Drink some water or you'll regret it in the morning."

Another hushed sound.

"But Ari, you know when I said ankles?" His voice had dropped an octave. "I really meant your tits."

"Oh my God." I laughed.

"Will you tell your boobs I'm sorry for ... for ... Ob. Jet, tit, fy... ing them." I laughed again. "Serious, Ari. Tits have feelings, too!"

"My boobs accept your apology." The stallholder smothered a smile. I cleared my throat. "I'll talk to you in the morning, okay?"

"Yeah, babe. I'm more than okay. I'm fucking great!"

His phone cut out. I shook my head and handed the shell to the stallholder.

"Couldn't help overhearing. Is this a present? Want it wrapped?"

"Yes, please."

"For someone special?"

"Yeah. He is." I handed over my money. "He's a good friend. Probably my best friend."

So many of my film and TV friends had disappeared from my messages and texts as soon as I started to travel after Wes. Film and TV were a fickle industry where we all clung to each other for news of more work and new projects, and as soon as we were not useful in scoring work, people who were once friends faded away.

I headed to the food trucks, bought noodles and watched the moon rise over the markets, thinking about what I'd said to Jet while he was drunk.

I traced a finger over the shell, sighing.

What was I doing? This wasn't a relationship.

Was it?

No, of course not. It was a friendship. A bit of fun. *He's drunk. He won't even remember in the morning.*

Why the hell do I feel sad? I pushed the question from

my mind, discarded my noodles in a bin and returned to Bessie, restless.

THE NEXT DAY AFTER ELEVEN, my phone buzzed with a rapid flood of texts.

Jet: oh man. I feel like shit

Jet: I noticed I called you last night. fuck, did I say anything embarrassing?

Jet: got texts here from Tom saying I made a fool of myself

Jet: We've been called in for a fire, looks bad.

Me: oh hey birthday boy

Jet: haha yeah.

Jet: I'm sorry I didn't tell you

Jet: don't do birthdays. Don't want anyone to feel obligated to do anything

Me: too late. I've already been to the post office and sent your present

Jet: I remember something strange about you sending me the ocean?

Me: yes! Remember anything else?

Jet: Also have a hazy memory of apologising to your boobs *facepalm emoji*

Me: LOL you did

Me: my boobs accepted the apology

> Jet: what else did I do?

I paused. I wanted to tell him what he'd said about his feelings for me and calling me his girlfriend, but I wasn't sure what kind of reaction I wanted. Laugh it off or own up to it?

It felt like I was holding onto a secret that everyone but Jet knew. Was he faking his memory loss? Did he really remember what he had said?

> Me: you were having a very good time.
> Promise me you'll stay safe with the fire

Dots appeared and disappeared for over a minute: an eternity in texting time.

> Jet: thank fuck

> Jet: I'm sorry for anything I did, just in case you're being polite

> Me: hey I have to go. All good

I threw my phone on the coach seat beside me. We were about to arrive at Kakadu in less than an hour. As much as I love Bessie, it was a pleasure to be driven somewhere and pay for the luxury of dozing in my seat.

Three days of sightseeing, sleeping with air-conditioning and an inner-spring mattress, and an ensuite. A pre-Christmas treat for myself. Off the grid, me and nature, and a tour group of thirty other people, mostly retirees, with at least seven other languages spoken.

Was I a coward for not telling him what he'd said?

Why did my impulse tour booking this morning feel like I was running away?

My phone pinged again just before we turned off for the visitor centre.

> Jet: you sure? Nothing else? Tom said I owe you an apology, and to make sure you're okay

> Jet: Fuck, Ari. I'm so sorry if I said anything that was out of line

"Ladies and gentlemen," the bus driver announced. "We have arrived at Kakadu National Park and will be parking shortly to meet your tour guide."

A pre-recorded message played in Japanese over the speakers as I stared at my phone.

We disembarked the coach and headed for the visitor centre. Such natural beauty around me—palm trees, gums, red dirt and twisted rocky outcrops—and yet I kept staring at a text from a guy.

I had one bar of mobile reception. The booking agent had warned me that mobile reception was patchy at best here. I began a draft message.

> Me: you said something last night about us. About your feelings for me. And I want to know more. I want you to tell me everything about what you meant.

Someone bumped me from behind, making me accidentally hit send, and I swore my heart stopped.

"Everything okay?" the bus driver asked.

"Y-yeah," I managed to stammer.

The blue line went across the screen, slowly and surely.

I huffed a cry upon seeing the 'message failed' alert come up in red.

"Okay, everyone!" The bus driver clapped and began giving instructions.

I hit delete and connected to the free wi-fi at the visitor's centre, which was worse than one bar of mobile reception, and tried another message.

> Me: Nothing was out of line.

This time, after thirty seconds, the message was delivered and then read.

> Jet: okay. Good. Have fun. And I'll be safe. Promise.

FOUR DAYS LATER, for Christmas Eve, I sat in the air-conditioning of the Darwin RSL with some of the other tour guests having a drink together when Jet texted a photo of the shell I posted to him.

> Jet: Fuck, Ari!

> Jet: you sent me the fucking ocean! the shell is amazing!

> Me: glad you liked it.

> Jet: you had your ear against this shell, didn't you?

I shivered. He'd put the shell against his ear, too.

> Ari: I did.

> Ari: had to check it was working LOL

Jet: Ari, I love this present

Jet: thank you

More goosebumps. For two whole seconds, I thought about sending my original text demanding to know more about his declaration.

Me: you're welcome, Jet *smiley face emoji*

Jet: bushfire is out in time for Christmas. Hope Santa finds you tonight

Jet: Wish there was a way for me to give you something for Xmas

Me: your thank you is all I need

Jet: I'm listening to the shell right now imagining I'm there

Me: can I call you tomorrow? After your family thing?

Jet: I'll make it happen

10

Jet
What's the best gift you've ever received?

"Hi Mum, Dad. Merry Christmas. Come in."

We all hugged in the entryway, and Mum slowly made her way down the hall, looking into the bedrooms, the lounge and the kitchen.

The house was just five rooms: a tiny cottage with two bedrooms at the front overlooking a small veranda, a kitchen and lounge at the back and a small bathroom wedged between the kitchen and the second bedroom, and a laundry under a roof out the back door.

"Place is looking very nice, Jethro," Mum said with a glowing smile.

I'd hastily cut a small white cedar sapling that had the shape of a Christmas tree and had it in a bucket with rocks beside the fireplace. Grandad had very old tinsel garlands and decorations in a box high up in the main bedroom's wardrobes, and the tree was cheerful in gold and sparkling red.

"Could be better but I've been helping the rural fire brigade with the bushfires this week."

My parents noticed my firefighter jacket and go-to back-pack with a helmet on a peg near the backdoor, ready for a callout. Their faces were a mix of fear and awe.

Joining a fire brigade was setting down roots, as was buying livestock and fixing fences.

"I'm so glad we got through on the highway today to see you and the old place." Mum looked about, touching pictures still on the walls where my grandfather had hung them. "You're taking care of it really well."

"Still needs lots of work." I was momentarily derailed by her compliment. "I'll get a power point installed outside for the caravan so you can plug in when you visit."

"We're off-grid," Dad said dismissively, but Mum gave him a pointed look. "I mean, that would be very good, son."

"How's fruit picking going?"

"Did capsicums around Bundaberg and tomatoes at a farm we know well. Heading to Coffs Harbour for the blue-berry season after New Year's."

"Good money in capsicums," Mum added. "Will help pay for a new awning on the van."

"What's wrong with it?"

"Oh, a support is bent after a big storm." She adjusted a mango that was just ripe in the fruit bowl. "I remember this bowl. Didn't think my dad still had it."

"Do you want it?"

"No, dear, it's fine. Nowhere to put it in the van."

To say we were not a sentimental family was an under-statement.

Mum headed to the lounge and noticed Ari's shell on

the fireplace mantle. "Oh, this is pretty. I don't recall Dad owning any shells before. Where did you get this?" Mum held it to her ear, and Ari's small card fell to the floor.

"Mum! Please, be careful."

"I know how to hold a shell, Jethro," she said dryly, picking up the card before I could reach it. "Oh. Who's Ari? Stan, Jethro got a present from a girl. And she signed the card with a love heart."

I snatched the card and shell and returned them to the mantle, my face hot. "That was private."

Mum beamed. "Have you got a girlfriend?"

"No," I said quickly. "Just a friend." *A lady friend.* "Ari's just a good friend."

"Will we see her on this visit?" Mum asked hopefully.

"No. No, she's ... away."

Mum gave Dad a bemused look and then looked under the wooden mantle. "Still here," she chuckled. "Have you discovered your mother's and aunt's vandalism when we were twelve?"

"What? No." I bent down and looked up, and sure enough, Mum's and Aunty Jenny's initials were carved into the wood.

"You rebels." I straightened with Mum. "Why didn't Aunty Jenny want to inherit this place or for her kids?"

Mum waved me off. "Dad left her some money and shares. She reassured me she didn't want the burden of trying to sell this place after years of Dad pottering about with no maintenance." Her hand flew to her mouth. "But it all looks very nice."

I snorted in a way not unlike Ari. "It does need mainte-nance. Fencing is first, and then I'll work on the house. The kitchen cabinets are held together with paint."

Dad huffed a laugh. "Don't miss having a place to

constantly upkeep. The van is doing well despite the storm."
Mum coughed into her hand and pointedly looked at Dad
again. "But yeah, the place looks good."

"Look, I get it. You're nomads. You like being on the
road."

Dad shrugged. "Very true. But what about you, son? You
were happy on your bike and working on sheep stations all
over the country. What's it like being stuck here?"

Part of me suddenly wished the curtains didn't have
holes or the laminate on the kitchen benches wasn't cracked
and chipped. Or that the paint wasn't peeling in one corner
of the kitchen.

But I didn't feel stuck at all and told them so. "I feel like
I'm making it better, slowly but surely. Learning heaps about
animal care. And being a caretaker. It's a learning curve."

"You never liked being on the road growing up. Not like
your brother. He happily settled into any new school or
distance education, but you hated leaving."

"I hated leaving my friends every six months and
routine." My tone was harsher than I'd intended.

Mum looked crestfallen while Dad looked like I'd
sprouted an extra head.

"I don't hold it against you. Sorry I said that."

"Don't be," Mum said softly. "I'm glad you said it. And
I'm glad you decided to give this place a chance. Why don't
you show us your weaners?"

Dad chuckled, and I shook my head, smiling as I led
them to the back door. "Never say it like that again, Mum."

CHRISTMAS WAS A LOW-KEY AFFAIR. My brother arrived just
before lunch, driving five hours after he finished his shift at

the mine. Any fears I had that my brother may have regretted being bought out of his inheritance were dispelled. Tully proudly showed us photo after photo of his new boat bought with the proceeds of buying him out, listing off stats and features.

I baked a ham in the BBQ, and didn't ruin it, following Ash's instructions to include pineapple and cloves and a glaze made with bourbon and marmalade, and it was a hit with the family.

The potato salad was also damn good, and there was none left for leftovers at dinnertime.

Tully and I took up our spots in Grandad's old wooden chairs while Mum and Dad staked a place around the bonfire site with their specialist camping chairs, and we enjoyed drinks watching the sunset.

Ari texted after nine when Mum and Dad had retired to their van. They couldn't even be tempted to sleep in the spare bedroom for a few nights. They were #vanlyf to the core, even if they had never heard of hashtags. Tully wanted to camp in his swag in the backyard, too.

Ari: Merry Christmas Jet

Ari: how are your parents?

Me: good, awkward, but good.

Me: loved your Kakadu photos earlier. Looked like a great trip

Ari: Tour was fantastic and worth every cent. But feels a bit weird catching up on the fires while I've been playing tourist. Cody sounded exhausted when I called the fam today. Almost wanted to drive back home to help.

Ari: But enough of fires, what did Santa bring?

Me: Ha. Mum found our old stockings in the linen cupboard and hung them on the fireplace. Now I know what the two random nails in the mantlepiece are for.

Me: she stuffed our stocking with chocolate, socks and jocks. And they gave me a new welcome mat for the front door. I think that makes me officially middle aged now?

Me: bro gave me a gift card.

Ari: hahaha! my fam gave me money since I'm way over here at the mo

Ari: Ash said she has a present for me when I get back.

Ari: My gifts haven't arrived yet, ugh. Glad you got my shell before Christmas. Ash is pregnant and both her and Cody are glowing. Bit of a bombshell dropped over the Christmas call. Going to be a low key courthouse ceremony after they see his family in Canada. They fly Boxing Day

Me: Not surprised to hear they are tying the knot. And that's awesome re Ash! Aunty Ari has a nice ring to it

Ari: it does. Of course now I have to buy all the cute baby things as I travel.

Ari: So, it was news to me: you and Ash text as well?

Me: we're colleagues, Ari ...

Ari: you've never mentioned it

> Me: I didn't? It's only been recent. Ash has been on my back to improve my home cooking. I baked a ham for Christmas dinner today and the fam said it was a success

> Me: and Mum saw your card and the shell and there was an inquisition about who Ari was

> Ari: Ohhhh what did you say?

> Ari: just a little something from my sext pal

She'd signed that card with a love heart with her name in it. Did that mean something more than sext pals?

> Me: the old mates at the pub call you my 'lady friend'

> Ari: hahaha! do they call your male friends 'man friends'?

> Me: I'm not sexting any of my man pals

> Ari: speaking of … do you have privacy tonight? Or are walls thin between you and your parents?

> Me: folks are retired to the van. Bro is camping in backyard. I have the place to myself. No baths while they are here but I'm in bed and alone

> Ari: video call or photos?

The idea of being busted by Mum and Dad coming into the house to use the bathroom while I had my dick in hand on a naked video call to Ari did not help set the mood.

> Me: what if we sent each other short videos?

> Me: send me a cheeky little striptease. I'll return one. I'll even wear my Santa hat.

Ari: Tis the season to strip in a Santa hat *winky face emoji*

Ari: I have one too from face painting at Christmas markets last week, and a pair of red undies I think you'll find intriguing

AFTER THIRTY MINUTES of exchanging messages and videos, I had to call and hear her voice. Hearing her breathy moan sent me over the edge, and I came, calling her name into my pillow.

We lay there, listening to each other breathe and to the sounds of the night: cicadas and a random bird out my window, and I could hear the ocean breaking on the shore in the background.

Ari broke the silence first. "I'll never look at a Santa hat the same way after those videos."

I loved how I could tell she was smiling from the tone of her voice.

I should clean up, but I just wanted to talk a little longer. "Really love the shell. I listened to the ocean this morning before anyone was up and thought of you."

Ari was silent for a long moment. "I'm so glad."

"Merry Christmas, Ari."

"It was very merry indeed."

It was now after ten, and I was exhausted. To all the tired mothers of Australia hosting Christmas on hot days with no air-conditioning and making a hot meal for their families, I salute you. You are all the MVP.

"Your camera angles were inspired tonight. I'm going to save tonight's efforts for future reference."

"Mmmmm and ditto re you."

I groaned, sticky from my release and the summer heat. "Gonna have to say goodnight and go have a quick shower."

Ari made a muffled noise and said something. *Holy shit.* Did she just say—

"What was that?" I sat up, fully alert. "Couldn't quite catch that."

"Mmmmm," she purred into the phone. "I said 'love your work'."

I let out a long breath, flopped back down on the bed and stared at the ceiling fan turning slowly. It really had sounded like she'd said ... but no. "Glad you approved."

"I'm going to sleep well tonight, thinking of you." She moaned again. "Night, Jet. And merry Christmas."

"Night, Ari."

11

Ari

True confessions: What is your most embarrassing dating disaster?

I entered the pub in Broome, freshly showered after three days away to the Dampier Peninsular on a 4WD tour. When I'd left, Ash and Cody were caught in a social media scandal involving Cody's old flame. Being without mobile reception in remote Australia had been so hard. Feeling so damn helpless that I couldn't do anything.

I ripped down a brochure from a noticeboard in the pub for surfing lessons on Cable Beach as several messages from Ash downloaded. She was now home, and had been back for days, but was startled from my messages to hear Ballydoon mentioned on the TV behind the bar.

"The small town of Ballydoon has become the epicentre for managing the bushfire response for the communities of the Greater Stanmore District, led by the acting rural fire brigade chief Ryan Turner." The camera went back to a journalist in a pristine white jacket. "An evacuation centre has been set up in the Ballydoon School of Arts hall for communities south of Ballydoon cut off from their homes as bushfires continue to keep the highway closed."

My heart pounded.

"An arsonist is believed to be behind the latest fires threatening homes. Police are continuing to investigate reports ..."

But they'd put out the fires just before Christmas. And it was all happening again, and worse, in the new year.

A new message from Ash pinged on my phone.

> Ash: you probably know by now, but yeah, there's more fires. They reckon someone around here is lighting them.

Oh God, Mum, Ash's house, my friends, Jet! Everyone I knew was in danger.

I immediately called Mum. Voicemail. I tried again and no answer. I left a message asking Mum to call me as soon as she could and hung up.

I dialled Jet's number, and I almost cancelled the call when he finally answered.

"Ari, hey."

"Oh my God, Jet! Is your house okay? What about your animals? What about you?" I practically yelled down the phone. Several patrons swivelled towards me.

"I'm okay, babe." He sounded so tired. "Animals are okay, for now. Neighbour's keeping an eye on them. How are you? You in Broome?"

"Who cares about me! Jet, are you going to lose your farm?"

"It's bad out there, not gonna lie, but the firefighters are amazing, and they're doing a great job; I'm safe, and that's what matters."

A sob escaped my lips.

"Fuck, are you crying? Ari, I'm okay, I promise."

"I just … thought I might have lost you."

He sighed. "I'm okay, baby. You're not going to lose me."

Hearing the smile in his voice gave me some comfort. "I wish I could hug you right now."

"Wouldn't say no to that." He chuckled. I heard my name and Jet's in the background. "Hey, it's your mum. Yeah, Debra, it's Ari. Sure, here you go."

"Ari! Darling! It's just madness here at the hall—"

"Mum! Where is your phone? I've called you twice, and you didn't answer!"

"I dropped it, and it's ruined now."

"Wait, why are you at the hall? Have you been evacuated too? Has something happened to Ash and Cody's house?"

"No! Good lord, dear! I'm helping with the Ballydoon Ladies Auxiliary. Making my famous beetroot salad for the evacuees and firefighters. We've got a roster for helping in the kitchen at the hall to do meals."

"You're cooking." Only God could save Ballydoon now.

"No need to sound so horrified, Ariane. You like my beetroot salad!"

"Put Jet back on, please, Mum."

Mum huffed but complied.

"Hey," Jet answered.

"You can't let her serve beetroot salad. It's just bloody awful. I mean, like so awful, you'd rather deal with the bushfires."

"You want me to stop your mum from serving salad?"

"It has tinned asparagus in it! Ash and I called it the stinky pee and poo salad because it makes, well, you know."

Jet laughed. "Asparagus and beetroot have a certain effect on the body."

"Yes! You can't let her serve that!" I waved around me. "You have to save the firefighters from Mum's helpfulness."

"You can count on me to save the brigade."

"You're still laughing, Jet!" I smiled. "So, can you still talk Saturday night?"

"Oh, talk." Jet's voice was deeper. "It's a little hard right now to be able to do that."

"You're in the evacuation centre?"

"No, I'm sleeping on Ash's couch while I'm cut off from home."

"What?"

"She insisted, even with their jet lag. They've been great. Cody's a great dude, too."

I huffed. He was more a part of my family than I was. "Well, I can't do our 'talk' either. I accepted a job offer. They want me to start tomorrow for five weeks."

"Wow, that's great, Ari. What are you going to do?"

"Don't laugh."

I had no idea why I was nervous. I hurriedly opened my photos and selected a grinning family in their country best: pressed shirts, Akubra hats, spotless jeans and boots. Four days ago, as I'd booked my last minute 4WD camping adventure, I'd found their job. I applied, and they rang within two hours asking if I'd do a video phone interview, and was offered the job to start after I came back from the Dampier Peninsula.

"I promise there will be no merriment."

I snorted and inhaled a deep breath. "Atemporarygovernessonaremotestation."

Jet softly chuckled again. "Can you say that once more with pauses between the words?"

"A nanny, like a governess. Their usual governess is away for a holiday, and they wanted someone to be with their three girls while they did station duties with reduced staff. I liked them and their girls, and they offered me the job on the spot."

The family was picture perfect for a boot company or country clothing ad, and they'd been so nice on the video call, even though it had dropped out three times during my interview.

Before Jet could react, I ploughed on. "I've been liking the face painting jobs with kids. And so did the station owners when I had my interview. The girls think I know lots of famous people because of my film and TV work. I thought I'd give this a try to see if it's something I like."

"That's awesome, Ari. Really proud of you." He paused, and then spoke closely into the phone. "Guess we have to play it by ear about when we can celebrate your new employment with a chat?"

"Yeah, we do. Not until I know what's happening with my sleeping quarters and proximity to three girls under the age of ten."

"Not that we can celebrate with me on Ash's couch."

I sighed, a little bewildered at how a one-night stand had become a weekly phone sex date who was currently sleeping on my sister's couch but also a friend. A really good friend.

My mind spiralled into freefall.

A really good friend who'd said he loved me when he was drunk.

I hugged my stomach tight. "I'm scared," I breathed, not sure I meant just the bushfire threat.

"I'm scared, too. It's serious shit out there," he whispered. "And your sister and Cody bang like bunnies, you know what I'm saying?"

I snickered. "Poor Jet."

"I sleep with earplugs but can still hear them going at it." Jet sighed. "I'm really glad you got the job, Ari."

"Yep. It's good. Yep."

"Is ... is everything okay?"

"I'm fine. Everything is fine."

"Right, Ari. You don't sound fine."

How did my one-night stand become central to looking after my family during an emergency?

"What are we exactly doing here, Jet?" My voice was high pitched and shrill. I stalked out of the bar and onto the street, looking this way and that for somewhere private.

"Um, talking?"

"That's not what I mean!"

"Then tell me what you mean, Ari."

"Why are you staying with my sister?"

"Ash and Cody said it was okay. And you know, cut off from my home in a national emergency."

"But why, Jet? You could have stayed somewhere else. With Tom Turner in his shearers' quarters. Even the pub." I ducked into a laneway beside the pub and paced in front of their bins.

"Well, I just ..."

"What! You just what?"

"I want to make sure your family was safe because I know you're feeling out of control that you can't help!"

"That's not true!"

"Ari, at Christmas, you wanted to drive back because you were so worried about them!"

The fact he was correct only ratcheted up my frustration. "Why do you care if my family is safe?"

"Because, of course I do, Ari!"

"But why? I mean, why do you talk to me each week? Why are we friends? What—"

"Because I care about you!" Jet's voice boomed down the phone. "I feel closer to you if I'm on the couch at your sister's making sure your family is okay. Is that so wrong?"

All I could hear in my mind was his voice, full of laughter and happiness on his birthday, screaming into the phone: *I love you, Ari! I love you!*

As he spoke, Jet's voice became so deep. "Because, Ari, for me, every Saturday when we talk, it's more than just fucking over the phone. I like you. A lot. And I thought—" He abruptly stopped.

I listened to his sharp breathing, waiting, and then caved. "What did you think?" I whispered, tears running down my cheeks.

"Never mind."

"Please tell me."

"I thought you cared about me, too," he croaked.

I sniffed. My tongue didn't work. *I care about you so much!*

"Jesus, Ari, you drive me crazy sometimes, but I care. So much."

"That wasn't meant to happen. This friendship between you and me."

I should just tell him I feel the same way about him. But I couldn't help myself—I wanted to bully him into revealing himself, knowing I was going to be cruel and take his beautiful words, smash them into tiny pieces, and then stomp on them.

Jet laughed without humour. "There were no rules about this. There never is with love."

That little four-letter word bounced around my brain

like a dropped drawer of cutlery, metallic sharp things ricocheting into dark places.

Butterflies soared in my stomach. A hot, ugly part of me, all slithering and slimy, made of lava and venom, had strangled my voice.

I didn't want to say the words he wanted to hear. *Couldn't.*

"Remember when you asked me a speed dating question in my kitchen? What was something I learnt from my mother? Well, I'll tell you now," I hissed. "I learnt early on not to rely on a man, that relationships end and promises of love are just a lie. I watched my dad leave his wife and daughters without a backward glance."

"I'm not your father, Ari. And I sure as hell am not Wes. So stop holding me to account for what they did."

"This isn't true love, Jet!" I spat. "It's not love at all!"

For the longest moment, no one said a word.

All I could do was huff out shuddering little breaths.

Deny my words, Jet. Say something!

"You're right," he finally said. "It's not."

Tears ran down my cheeks. *If he loved me, he'd fight for me right now, wouldn't he?*

I felt like I'd been stabbed in my stomach. I wanted to sink to the ground, beside the stinking mess of the bins and dissolve into the dirt.

But why would he fight for me when I wasn't fighting for him?

"You made that clear right at the start. I'm sorry I said that." He made a noise. Sniffing? Was he crying? "I have to go, Ari."

"Good."

Neither of us hung up.

But then I caved, one last hit of vitriol. "I'm going on a date anyway."

"A date?" Jet's voice was so quiet I could barely hear him.

"Yeah. A date."

"Right. I'll let you go, then. Enjoy your date."

The phone went dead.

I ran all the way back to the van and shut myself inside, locking out the world.

12

Ari

Sweet or Spicy: What's the most impulsive thing you've done?

It took all of twenty minutes to match with someone on an app and agree to meet for a drink at dusk.

So what if I'd lied to Jet? It wasn't a lie now, I thought, slamming Bessie's door to head out to meet someone at Cable Beach.

Even though it was the wet season, there were lots of single men on holiday in Broome, looking to find single women on holiday as well. Some were tourists, others FIFO workers looking to hook-up before their next shift. Hugo, my match, was the latter.

We'd agreed to meet at a beachfront bar overlooking Cable Beach. The owners had converted a vintage caravan into a mobile bar with outdoor chairs and bean bags and oversized games like chess and Jenga.

It was a simply stunning location under palm trees, with

the sun turning gold across the sea and distant clouds ballooning for a possible storm later. It was too early for the camel tours, but they'd be here soon.

I pulled out my phone, acknowledging compliments about Bessie to a few passing tourists and walked over to the edge of the grass to take a photo of the famous beach to send to Jet.

Nausea was an instant ache in my stomach.

I lowered my phone. This date was wrong. Of course it was. I was the biggest idiot in Australia.

I pivoted to leave.

Hugo had sent some interesting messages as I'd driven to meet him here. Cheesy lines about going back to his dorm for a good time and had added not one but two dick pics to ensure he was absolutely clear about what he was hoping would come later.

Why had I even told Jet I was going on a date when I had no intention of doing it whatsoever? Why had I acted on my impulsive rage? I prickled and itched all over like I didn't fit in my own skin. What the hell was wrong with me?

I staggered away from the grass edge, my stomach rolling, and barrelled into a man.

He caught me by the elbow. "Ari?"

I blinked, glancing up.

"Hey, thought it was you." He looked me up and down and grinned. "Hugo. From online."

"Oh. Sorry, this was a mistake."

"Excuse me?"

"I'm going. Sorry. I didn't mean to do this."

I pushed past him, and then Hugo shouted after me. "Fucking cock tease."

Ignoring the looks from some of the seated guests, I

quickly made my way to Bessie, climbed in and shut the door with the windows up despite the stifling heat.

Who was I kidding? It was an oven.

I turned over the engine and drove off with a squeal of tyres, mildly satisfied that Hugo was being escorted out of the mobile bar serving area by two waitstaff.

I drove to the other side of Broome and parked with a waterfront view of Dampier Creek, got out and strolled along the jetty path, and then messaged Ash.

> Me: Tried to go on a date

> Me: Didn't work out

> Me: Don't even know why I tried. Feel incredibly stupid, sick, embarrassed

> Me: are you up?

> Ash: Greetings from the land of fire. Seriously bushfires suck. I just puked from morning sickness so you have me alone for at least ten minutes while I'm on a break at work.

> Ash: why are you panicking over a date?

> Ash: Wait, are you in trouble?

My phone rang.

"Hey, Ash. I'm okay. I'm safe." I sighed. "Although he was a complete douchebag."

"What's going on?"

"I was talking to Jet. Okay, it was a fight. An argument. And I said I was going on a date, even though I wasn't, but then I got on an app and matched with someone here in Broome and agreed to meet him out of spite."

"There's a lot to unpack there," Ash said carefully. "Why would you do that?"

"Jet said he loved me."

Ash sighed. "The stupidity is rapidly escalating in this story."

I ignored my sister's sarcasm and continued my tale of woe. "Jet was drunk when he said it, and I don't think he remembers but I sometimes wonder if he does. But tonight he said he really cared for me. Not like just friends, you know? Made me realise things between us crossed a line a long time ago and it needed to stop."

"This might be my pregnancy hormones speaking—" Ash paused—"but none of that made any sense."

I huffed and kicked at the sand.

"You've been sending him postcards for months. They're all over the bar at work. How long has this thing been going on?"

I sighed. "It's not a thing. But we've been texting for months. Since Mum's speed dating night last year."

"Ari, that's like seven months!"

I groaned. "I know."

"What exactly do you mean 'you crossed a line'? Are you guys doing more than talking and texting?"

"So much more," I muttered.

"He raved at work about a shell you sent him."

"It was one gift one time."

"That arrived before Christmas, before your family's gifts." Ash sniffed. "Not that I care, but I'm just saying."

"Luck of the postal service," I retorted.

"We love the baby onesie with the whale shark on it. Thank you." Ash sniffed. "You have two minutes of my time left. May I point out that you share yourself with him. More than anyone else, I'm guessing?"

I groaned again. "You can't say anything to him about this at work."

"Course not. Sisters have a right to silence and to protect family. Can I also add it's not like we have a staffroom here where we all gossip about the girl that Jet is texting and getting postcards from? Although the old fellas in the bar love your travel updates."

Ash was silent for a moment, possibly drinking water. "So why did you go on a date?"

"I don't know," I whined. "I just said it while fighting with him, and then I opened an app and matched up with someone."

"Come on, Ari. Think. Why the hell would you do that?"

"Because he's in love with me and I'm not."

"And that was your mature way as a friend to clarify your relationship with him?"

She had me there. "How did you know Cody was the one?"

"You have like thirty seconds left and you ask me that?" Ash inhaled deeply. "It felt right with Cody in a way that I'd never felt with anyone else. But Ari, how I feel about Cody isn't the answer about you and Jet."

For once, I let the silence settle. She was right.

"Would you come to my wedding?"

"Oh, I—"

"I'd really like my sister here. You understand about what it was like when Dad left us, and now here I am about to get married, of all things. Please say you will."

"I—I don't know."

"Cody will pay for your flights. A quick in and out trip for the wedding, and then you'll be back to Bessie and your lap around Australia. It's hardly cheating."

A tight knot of anxiety niggled in my belly.

"You're worried you'll see him, aren't you?"

My anxiety spiked. "Jet's invited?"

"Well, I invited everyone at work. I mean, Ryan and I have worked together for years, and John has been an amazing boss and yeah, I like Jet. He's cool. Wait, have you talked to him and explained yourself for your dumb actions?"

"No."

"Then you are being a coward, Ari. A big coward. Call the man and make this right."

"I'm not a coward! I just don't know what to say!"

"Start with sorry. Now, I'm hanging up on you and returning to make the best chicken parmis Ballydoon has ever seen feeling like a bilious whale. I am ending this call by saying, with honesty and love, that you are a dumbass."

Ash hung up, and I stood looking out at the marina and knew she was right.

13

Jet

Deal-breaker: What does keeping house mean for you?

Blake stuck out like a sore thumb yet again in the middle of my kitchen, like he didn't know whether to stand or sit. Like he didn't know how to be a guest in someone's house. He glanced around at every flat surface covered in bowls, glasses, saucepans and baking trays, and every item that had been crammed into the pantry.

"Found some spices dating back to 1997," I said by way of explanation for the cleaning frenzy in the kitchen. "Doing a big clean-out. Getting this place sorted."

Blake looked mystified. Everything he owned was packed on the tray of his ute. He didn't need cumin or bay leaves or even a spice rack.

My phone pinged several times with messages.

Blake picked up my phone before I could reach it. "Huh, Ari is sure apologising hard to you."

Curiosity urged me to snatch my phone off Blake and read what she'd said. I took two steps forward, shook my head and paced away.

"What's going on?" Blake asked.

"Nothing."

Blake made a game show buzzer noise for an incorrect answer and rolled his eyes. "Try again. What is going on?"

"I met someone at the speed dating night."

He said nothing at first and then rolled his eyes again. "Ari."

I blinked. "Yes."

"You've got her postcards up at the pub." He waved to the fridge where I had her apology postcard from Broome tacked up with several magnets. "And the shell over the fireplace. And the fact that you bleated out that you loved her on your birthday."

I sunk into a kitchen chair. "I did what now?" My voice was nothing more than a hoarse whisper.

"You don't remember? You called her and everything."

"Fuck."

"This calls for beers." Blake opened the fridge and plonked a cold one in front of me. "What's she apologising for?"

"She wants to be friends."

Blake shrugged. "So, find another girl."

"Blake, I don't want to go find another girl. I like the idea of having a girlfriend. I want to be with someone who likes me as much as I like them."

My best friend's face screwed up in horror. "Like, only be with one woman?"

"Yes, mate. Have you ever thought how amazing that is? Someone choosing you out of everyone else? And you choosing them?"

Blake scoffed. "Have you not heard how amazing having sex with lots of women, some at the same time, if possible, is?" He grinned and tilted his head, looking at me as if seeing me for the first time. "You really like this Ari, don't you?"

I couldn't hold back a heavy sigh. "Yeah."

"Shit, you're gone. She's got you by the balls."

"If only," I muttered. "I don't know how to be just friends with her."

Blake frowned. "Isn't she halfway around the country?"

"Practically, yeah."

"So what are you going to do to convince her to be with you?"

"Aren't you going to convince me I should just fuck other women until I forget about her?"

Blake shrugged. "Last year, I would have. But you've been different since that speed dating night when you met her."

"She wants to be friends, and as much as I want more, and told her that, it's not changing. She's not even here!" I laughed without humour. "So I am the one who needs to move on."

"I'm sorry, man."

The old clock in the lounge counted the seconds of silence.

"You know, your grandfather bailed me up in this kitchen after we'd been arrested and then let out on bail into his care. You'd gone to bed, but he had words with me in here."

"What the fuck?" I sat up straight. "You've never said a thing about that."

Blake shrugged. The movement was anything but casual.

"What did he say?"

"Told me to lift my game and make better choices. That he knew I didn't have family. That I was always welcome here as a place to call home." Blake glanced around. "Being your friend probably did save me, you know?"

"He ripped me a new one that night, too. Told me I was going to learn to be a better man."

Blake grinned. He glanced around the room again and shook himself. "Feels weird being here, like I can just see your grandad out the corner of my eye, walking in from the paddocks. He'd love how you are all tied up over a girl."

I smiled in spite of myself. Blake was right.

"What would your grandfather tell you to do about Ari?"

I took a large swallow of my beer, relishing the bitter aftertaste. "Might see her at Ash's wedding in a month. Maybe I won't go. Maybe I will, and we will be just friends again."

I drained my beer as thunder rumbled, as if right on cue, ominous and foreboding. The wind had picked up, and there was a flash of lightning and the lights went out.

Blake sighed. "Well, I'm not driving out in a storm, so I guess you're stuck with me for another night."

I flicked on the battery-operated camping lantern. "I'll cook something on the barbeque after you sort out Tupperware lids and bases while I get onto saucepans."

Blake barked a laugh as he got up and retrieved more beers from the fridge. "No way, mate. I'm going to drink your beer and watch you play house by candlelight."

~

Ari

. . .

I FUMED and paced in front of my van. Why wouldn't he respond to my texts? Maybe he was working. When had that ever stopped him? I eventually gave up wearing a groove in the grass in front of my van, flopped into my camp chair and called my mum.

"Debra, speaking!" she trilled.

"Mum, it's Ari."

"Yes, I know, dear. Your name comes up on my phone when you call." I rolled my eyes, as she asked, "so, what's wrong, then?"

"Why would you assume something is wrong?"

"Because you're grunting at me, dear." Mum huffed. "It's not ladylike, either. So, what's wrong?"

I leapt out of my camp chair, throwing a hand into the air. "Men are what's wrong!"

Somewhere in the distance, someone yelled, "Amen, sister!"

"Oh yes, men." Mum sighed. "They're all like your father, you know. Love you and leave you."

"Not. Like. That," I snapped.

"Except Cody, of course. He proved he is the exception." Mum sighed. "Well, what is your man issue? Don't tell me another one cheated on you."

"No!" I licked my lips. "Why, do you know if Jet has seen other women while I've been gone?"

"Ah. So this is about young Jethro."

It seemed my dumbassery was continuing. It was on the tip of my tongue to demand Mum tell me everything she knew about Jet's love life when I stopped myself in time, making a gargling sound.

"Are you alright, dear?"

This was nonsense thinking; we were not a couple; we slept together one night, and he could see whoever he wanted. So can I.

"He's interfering with what I want to do with my life, and he has no right!"

"Is this about Wes? Is he harassing you? I swear to God, if I see his perfectly styled hair again, I'll throw so much bleach on him, his hair will fall out—"

"No, Mum! Not Wes! And no bleach attacks, thank you." I sucked in a breath. "What do you mean, 'again'?"

"That so-called actor has now turned to 'journalism', if that's what you call it."

I opened my mouth to demand my mother explain herself but she continued. "He was doing special coverage of the fires here, interviewing locals, that sort of thing. The Turner family have been on TV recently, and there's nation-wide attention on Ballydoon, so much so, Wes Schumacher has been in town."

"Huh."

And there it was: nothing. No anger, no vitriol. Just a whole lot of ... nothing.

"But don't worry, dear. After Jet spoke to him, I told him I would hunt him down and leave him hairless. His whole body, devoid of hair."

There was a lot to unpack in that statement. "J-Jet spoke to him?"

"Yes, Wes tried to ask him a question on live TV, and Jet told him, well, Jet strongly hinted at a specific kind of fornication that Wes should engage in, and walked off, leaving Wes gaping like a goldfish on national TV."

I huffed a laugh.

"It's become a meme online. You should look it up. Now, who is it interfering with your life?"

I clamped my lips shut, not wanting to say his name again for some reason. "Just ... someone."

"Speaking of what to do with your life, you can always join me here in the salon and be the beauty therapist."

"Mum." I scrubbed my face.

"You're wasting your life in that van."

"I'm not wasting my life! I'm finding out what I want to do with it."

"Beauty therapy in a country town with your hair stylist mother is a respectable career choice."

Everyone was interfering with my life choices. "I have my own ideas of what I want to do."

"Oh? And what are these ideas, Ari? Because all I've heard is you've got ideas, not what they are."

"I ... just ..." I wasn't ready. Not just yet. "I can't tell you right now."

"Well. Maybe we *are* just trying to help." Mum huffed. "What's so wrong about that? Especially as you haven't shared with your mother what you want to do."

I took a deep breath. Maybe Jet was helping, not interfering. And even Mum, in her perverse kind of way?

Wes had undermined and discouraged me from doing different things with my life and always steered me to do the things that helped his career.

Could I tell the difference between helping and interfering?

"I just ... I like the idea of ..."

"Yes?" I could hear Mum's false nails clacking on the salon counter, waiting for me to speak. "You're almost there. Spit it out."

"Kids." Mum made a garbled noise, and I laughed. "I'm not pregnant, too, Mum. I meant I'd like to work with kids. Like, I dunno. Childcare. Or ... teaching."

"Teaching?" Her nails stopped. "Like going to university?"

I waited for Mum to say more but silence filled the conversation.

"Yeah, teaching," I said, giving into the void. "I saw an ad for a nanny on a cattle station, and I applied and got it and start tomorrow. It's four weeks, maybe as long as six, so the regular nanny can have a holiday, and I'm going to try it and see if I like it. I know it's not a classroom or childcare centre or anything, but I'd be helping the kids with some school-work at the end of the contract and doing activities with them. If I don't like this kind of work with three kids, I figure I won't like it with twenty-five in a classroom."

I sucked in air, feeling giddy for finally admitting to my mother my fresh and new career interest.

"I think you'd be a great teacher, Ariane." Mum's voice was almost a whisper.

"Really?"

"You always had a talent with children. And you're a smart girl. You can do more than pull beers and paint faces at fetes." I could imagine Mum holding up a pointed finger in the air, commanding my silence from afar. "*Not* that anything is wrong with that, but you have more to offer in the world."

I sobbed, gulping air, and covered it up pretending to cough. Wes told me once I wasn't smart enough to get into uni. No one in our family had gone to university. Somehow, that had got under my skin as something I couldn't do. Would never do.

To have someone say I'd be good at something was a huge relief and overwhelming.

"Your road trip got me thinking about how I ran off to Darwin as soon as Ash finished school and you settled in Sydney. I just had to get away from the town that still asked after my ex-husband, even though it had been years since he'd stepped foot into our house and lives. And I'm glad I sold up the salon in Darwin and came back. Because I came back as Debra, not some man's wife."

"I walked past it last week. Recognised the shop front from the photos you sent. Salon has a new name, though."

"Good for them. My business is doing very well here, too. Especially when I find a beauty therapist. Doing country wedding packages is what clients want. I had Rosie Zanetti in here the other day. The Zanettis have big plans for that winery of theirs. And I've heard rumours the Turners next door are going to get into tourism and events, too. And we'll be ready with our wedding packages for hair and make-up."

Mum sounded so happy, so excited for her future.

"Ari, I ran to Darwin to find myself. Much like how you were driving off into the sunset away from Wes."

"I wasn't driving away from Wes, I was getting away from make-up and the salon. I needed space to figure out who I was if I wasn't in film and TV holding a make-up brush."

"And have you found that answer yet?"

"I've found something I think is worth exploring."

"Now that's great to hear. If I may say something, know when it's time to come back."

"How do you know?"

"That's on you, dear. And you may not even feel like you're one hundred percent ready but that you're enough. That you are more brave than scared."

"Okay." It was now dark. "I should go. Gotta pack and get ready for an early morning start to meet the cattle station owners. I'm going to drive with them to their place."

"I can't wait to hear all about it. Knock 'em dead, my dear."

14

Ari

Deal-breaker: What are your thoughts and beliefs about marriage?

It had been three weeks since our fight.

I'd written Jet an apology on my last Broome postcard on my first night at the cattle station. Posting it had been delayed by a week due to the monsoon finally arriving in earnest, leaving sealed and dirt roads flooded and the land drenched.

The rains also meant limited internet. And with every break in the weather, I'd get updates on Ash's wedding plans, how it wasn't a simple ceremony at the courthouse but a full blown big dress and guests at the chapel in Ballydoon, and a big reception. It sounded like the whole of Ballydoon was going. Except me.

And sneaking a look at Jet's social media feed. Photos of

him with his parents and brother on the veranda of his little farmhouse. A cranky tabby cat missing a chunk from its ear. A picture of his bonfire at night.

No women, though.

Mum was offering a free wash, cut and blow-dry for all firefighters and evacuated locals after the bushfires. Her post had even been shared by celebrities.

And I'd caught a reel that had gone viral of Mum throwing her beetroot salad over Wes' head. The look of horror on his face as the maroon juices trickled down his face and shirt made me think perhaps her salad wasn't so bad after all.

But all of the viral posts, social media scandal and wedding prep couldn't distract me enough from the fact I hadn't heard from Jet.

I'd written a short letter apologising for being mean and that, most of all, I wanted to be friends.

The postal service website said it could take seven to twelve business days to arrive. So there was like a ninety percent chance he had received my letter.

Or not.

With three girls under ten years old, we'd embraced Disney movies during the rains, as well as visits to their favourite swimming hole to cool off, answered thousands of questions about working in film and TV, and made scripts and videoed their own princess movies.

I even got them started on their schoolwork at the end of January.

It was the fifth of February, less than two weeks until Ash's wedding, and I still hadn't given her an answer if I was coming back.

As I made coffee before breakfast, my phone pinged.

> Ash: Hey, checking in about the wedding after our call.

> Ash: I'm sorry I hung up on you. And I know you haven't given me a real answer yet if you'll come home for the wedding … but … I wanted to ask you if you'd be my maid of honour

Holy shit, maid of honour!

> Ash: Cody says hi. wants to know how *his* van is doing.

I chuckled.

> Ash: but seriously, maid of honour: you in?

I quickly typed back a reply.

> Me: what about Flo, your bestie? I thought she was going to be your MOH

> Ash: she's a bridesmaid. But I want my sister to be my maid of honour and Flo is totally fine with that

> Ash: Mum is insisting she is doing my hair and I think I may actually kill her

> Ash: I'm not asking you to do my make-up. I just want the Wilde Women to be free of working at the wedding.

I felt a wave of relief I wasn't expecting. But if Ash had asked me to do it, I would have said yes. For her, it wasn't work.

> Me: if I come, I'll do it

> Ash: is that a weird way of saying you are coming to my wedding?

> Ash: you know I'm not intending on having another wedding in my lifetime, so if you want to see me do the deed, you'd better come

> Me: I'll think about it

> Ash: while you think about it, I'm emailing you your flight details so you can fly in and fly out. I've already bought the tickets

MIDMORNING, I called Ash on video chat.

"Please tell me you are calling to say you are confirmed as coming to my wedding." I cringed, and Ash rolled her eyes. "It's him, isn't it?"

"Who?"

"You are such a dumbass. I thought older sisters were meant to be the mature ones, but here we are." She inhaled a dramatic breath, flicking hair from her face. "I mean Jet, you idiot."

I sighed. "Sort of." Ash sighed, but I cut her off. "I called for another reason."

"Which is?"

"I asked you before about how you knew Cody was right for you."

"You did."

"So ... how did you?" I implored.

Ash cleared her throat. "I had to learn twice that he was for me. I had to believe what we had was stronger than the online hate of strangers. And stronger than doubt. And that we were going to be a family." She touched her belly, perhaps as a reflex. "It was tough, but it was more than worth it in the end."

A freak accident while on duty as a firefighter had cost Ash all her memories of Cody. They'd rebuilt their relationship from scratch, and Ash decided to take a second chance on him. And now they were getting married.

"I wrote Jet a letter apologising, but I haven't heard a thing since. It's been two weeks since I posted it and not a word. I practically begged him to be my friend after being so awful to him."

"What if he can't be friends with you because he's in love with you?"

"I don't want to lose my friend."

"You might not have a choice if it's too hard for him to be your friend when he knows you don't love him back. That's not fair at all." My body slumped. "My God, look at you. Let me put it this way. How has it felt all these weeks not talking to Jet?" Ash asked.

"Awful, like a part of me was missing." I took a deep breath. "When I talked to him, I felt I could do anything. And that scared me, but it scares me more not having him in my life."

"Shit."

Ash was looking at her screen, but not at me. "What?"

"Nothing," Ash said too quickly, rapidly pressing buttons.

"What is it?" I demanded again.

She sighed. "I just got a message from Mum. Jet is helping her with her Valentine's Day speed dating event."

"She's organised a speed date event the night of your wedding?"

"It's the night before, on the thirteenth. She's planned this thing where everyone ends up matched for dinner for two the next night on Valentine's Day at the pub. And John ends up with guaranteed dinner bookings with a set menu which I planned."

"And Jet's helping Mum? Like, as an assistant or like going as a participant to her speed dating event?"

"I'm not sure."

I don't know when I stood, but I swiped over to my social media app, found Mum's event and clicked on those who were going.

Jethro Cummings was listed first as attending.

I reached for the wall to steady myself.

"Ahh," Ash said slowly. "I can tell by the look on your face that you've seen it too."

"What if I did come home?"

Ash shrugged. "Then you'd be back home."

"I mean, what if I went home and faced Jet? What if I go all the way home and it doesn't work out?" My chin trembled. "What if Jet and I try a relationship and we break up and—"

"No." Ash pointed right down the barrel of her phone's camera lens. "No, nope, zilch, nada. It doesn't work like that. You need to decide that he's worthy of you. That he's worthy of your love." Ash's tone brooked no argument. "You need to commit to wanting to make it work. And if it doesn't, then that's sad and shitty, but I'm here for you, and so's Mum, in her own weird, intense way. And Cody, too. You've got a team who will catch you if it all goes wrong. Hell, you've got a whole town behind you, sis, but ..."

"But?"

"Does it feel like it would work out?"

"It feels so right. It feels wrong not having him in my life," I whispered. "And the thought of any other woman with their hands on him makes me want to scratch their eyeballs out."

Ash chuckled. "Now that's a Wilde woman talking. Then you know what you have to do, sis."

"I do. But ... I can't fly back for the wedding and then fly back here to keep doing my lap of Australia."

Ash frowned. "That's how return flights work. You fly in and then fly back."

"No, silly. I *have* to drive!"

"You are *literally* on the other side of the country to Ballydoon. How long is that going to take?"

I madly swiped to my maps app and gasped, breaking out in a cold sweat. "Okay, okay. More than five thousand kilometres away. It's like over seventy hours of driving. And I have nine days to do it in a 1970s Kombi van with no fuel injection or turbo power. But I have to show him I'm back, like really back."

Ash grinned. "So, what are you going to do?"

"Buy fuel and snacks in Broome and drive like hell."

"That's my sis. Go get your man."

I KNOCKED GENTLY at the station owners' office door where Marla was sorting invoices.

"You need to go, don't you?" Marla said, not looking up.

"I'm so sorry. I can't stay the extra week."

Marla smiled kindly, placing the paperwork down. "Don't be. We had a feeling something was going on back home. Other than your sister's wedding."

"I feel so bad about leaving the girls and you without help."

"More storms are coming, according to forecasts, so we won't be out much with the roads cut. We will be fine until their usual nanny comes back."

The girls crowded me in the office doorway.

"It's about true love, Mum," Edie said gravely.

"We heard everything." Piper grinned.

"You were listening to my calls?" I asked, horrified.

"Your sister called you a coward," Jodie whispered.

"Girls!" Marla looked alarmed.

"In a way, my sister was right. I was a coward." I shrugged. "No princess in a fairytale would hide from finding out if it's true love." I offered Marla a sheepish smile. "It's my fault. We've been down a princess fairytale rabbit hole since I arrived."

"No one does stories like Ari," Edie sang to the familiar tune. "No one finds true love like Ari!"

"Look, we suspected things at home were going to call you back earlier than we'd agreed," their mother said sheepishly. "We can fly you out in two days to Broome on our grocery run—"

"I need to drive Bessie back. Immediately."

Marla's eyebrows shot up.

"In that van?" Piper blurted, screwing her face up in doubt, hands on hips. "Good luck to ya."

"I've already googled the route, and it's at least seventy-three hours of driving." I licked my lips. "Without traffic or roadworks, or hold-ups."

Marla and I both glanced at the calendar hanging in her office. It was February the fourth. Nine days until the speed dating night.

"There are storms coming in this arvo. You'd have to leave right now. Jimmy is taking the truck with some steers to Broome any minute now. I was about to give him some invoices to hand over at the saleyards. You could follow him and hope you don't get bogged. Even for a monsoon season that's been quite dry by normal standards, it's plenty muddy on the roads."

"Shit." The girls giggled behind me. "Sorry, sorry. I just need to do this. I do need to go."

Their mum nodded. "We'll survive until their nanny comes back. And we won't get in the way of true love. Will we, girls?"

The girls watched me shove my belongings into bags and then eyed off my make-up stash with envy. So I surprised them by giving them sealed eye shadow, foundation powders and lipsticks, and several spare unused brushes as parting gifts.

Their dad had a spare jerry can of fuel filled, just in case.

Marla handed me bottled water, sandwiches, home-made muesli slice, a slab of cake and fresh tea in my thermos.

"Thank you for giving me the chance."

"Ari, you should know, if we didn't already have a nanny, we would have loved to have kept you on, if you would have had us. You were so good with the girls."

"Thank you so much. For everything."

"Good luck with this lad." Marla winked. "And your sister's wedding."

"So romantic," Edie swooned.

I was swamped with a group hug from the girls, who already had smears of electric blue eye shadow across their eyes.

"Can you send photos of the wedding, please?" Piper asked. "If you make it in that heap of junk."

I clutched my chest in faux shock. "Bessie is a classic, and she will make it, as will I."

"Alright, girls. Let Ari go. Or the storms are going to catch her and Jimmy on their way to the coast."

15

Ari—nine days later
Sweet or Spicy: What is your most favourite romantic scene in a
movie or book, and why?

I shambled into the pub, wiping my sweaty palms on my denim skirt.

Jet sat a table to the side, the pre-Valentine's speed dating night in full swing all around him. Love hearts hung from the ceiling, and a pink, red and white balloon arch greeted patrons at the door. Mum had vomited Cupid everywhere in the Ballydoon pub, yet again.

My back ached. My legs ached. My shoulders ached. Pretty sure my hair ached.

But seeing him sitting at a table all by himself, head down and picking at the corner of a beer coaster, it was my heart that hurt the most.

I'd driven for nine days straight. Two flat tyres, road-works everywhere, at least ten hours of driving a day, and some days more to make up for lost time dealing with the flat tyres and hold-ups. I almost cried seeing the retro Vegas-style Ballydoon sign on the highway and parked with a small screech of Bessie's tyres at the Ballydoon pub.

Journey over.

And just in time.

I was a wreck. Stained tee shirt, denim skirt and thongs. Hair was a ratty mess.

This would be so much better if I could have a quick shower and get some new clothes.

It was then that Jet looked up. "Ari?" he called, standing up and striding towards me. Jet came to a halt in front of me, looking me up and down. "It's really you. Are you wearing my tee shirt? From the first speed dating night?"

I bunched the hem in my fist. "Oh, yes. I found it after you left. So I stole it. Sorry."

He huffed a laugh, but his smile faded. "You're here."

"Singles night. Wouldn't miss it."

He snorted and shoved his hands into his jeans' pockets. "You're back for the wedding."

"That, and I'm here to meet someone special," I continued. "Not a hook-up."

"Someone special?" He eyed me warily.

I nodded. "Specifically, someone I need to apologise to. I'm hoping someone might give me a second chance."

His nostrils flared.

"I drove for nine days. I'm back. The road trip is over."

Still, Jet said nothing.

"I prepared questions along the way." I hastily pulled four slightly warped postcards from my back pocket from Karratha, Wudinna, Broken Hill and Narrabri. Jet stared at the postcards in my trembling hands. "I bought a postcard every time I stopped for petrol on my way here and wrote a question on each. I couldn't send them because I wanted to make sure I had them when I got here."

He looked up, his eyes fierce and sad—no, something else. *Hope*. My heart soared. I had to do this right. Everything came down to these four cards.

"K-karratha question." My voice wavered. "Do you believe in second chances?"

Something changed in his eyes: they were softer, a sparkle. "For the right person, I do."

I nodded. *Fuck, was I the right person?* "Good, good. Okay. Wudinna question." I flipped over the photo of the second largest rock in Australia after Uluru and read my scrawl. "I looked at the moon and the stars every night I was on the road and thought of you. Wudinna was the last clear night I had. Did you look into the night sky and think of me?"

He took a half step closer. "Every night, Ari."

I nodded again, swiping at the corner of my eyes. "Okay, great."

He chuckled. "You don't have to—"

"Yes, I do," I squeaked. "So just listen."

"Okay, go on."

"Broken Hill question." I sucked on my lips. "I haven't been with anyone since you." I stopped. In my exhaustion, I'd forgotten about this question. It wasn't fair to expect that he'd not seen anyone while I'd been gone. Of course, he was allowed to see others. I'd meant to tear it up and toss this postcard.

"Keep going," he urged, his voice hoarse.

"I shouldn't—"

"Ask."

I nodded and metaphorically pulled up my big girl pants. "It did feel to me like our friendship was more. To have kissed or slept with anyone else felt like ... cheating on you."

We'd never had any expectation at all about us being exclusive. Regret made my stomach lurch. I screwed up the postcard. "I can't ask this. It's not right to even expect—"

Jet reached out and gently peeled back my fingers, smoothing the postcard. "I never slept with anyone while you were gone, Ari. Even after our fight. It felt wrong to me, too."

A cry of relief escaped my lips. I brushed a tear from my cheek. "Oh."

Jet had moved closer still, but the only place where we touched was his hand covering mine and the Broken Hill postcard.

"You got one more question?" he asked, his breathing heavier.

I cleared my throat. "Narrabri question. I think I've been in love with you the whole time. But I wasn't ready to face what I was feeling." I couldn't look up from the postcard, couldn't risk seeing his reaction. "Were you really in love with me, too?"

"No."

My head snapped up. "What? Are you kidding me?"

He chuckled again, his eyes sparkling. "Not 'were' in love with you, Ari. I *am* in love with you. I never stopped."

I slapped the postcard against his chest. "I thought you were dumping me!"

He caught me by the wrist and hauled me against him. "You obviously didn't get my letter."

"What letter?" My heart was pounding. Was I having a stroke?

"I wrote back to you asking if we could be friends."

"What did you say?"

"I said I couldn't be just your friend when you had my heart. And I'd wait for you, if time is what you needed. And if you didn't love me, I'd let you be, and I'd do my best to be the friend you needed."

"I need you now. I need all of you."

He pressed his mouth to mine. I gasped in surprise, and he seized the opportunity to sweep his tongue over mine.

I dropped the postcards and wrapped my arms around his neck, deepening the kiss.

Our bodies moulded into each other, mine lighting up as his hands slid over my skin, holding me to him. Every call, every video chat, every filthy text: none of it compared to kissing him, touching him, feeling the way his body responded to mine.

I was about to climb him like a tree when someone started clapping and making cooing noises to my right. We broke apart to find my mother bouncing with glee.

"Oh! Have to say, I'm quite the matchmaker!" Debra waved jazz hands at the speed daters, beaming her white teeth to all. "May you all find love tonight!" She gestured to Jet and me just as I was sliding down the front of him in horror. "My speed dating nights are successful in helping people find love!"

"How close is Bessie right now?" Jet whispered.

"Car park."

"Go," he grunted, with a subtle thrust of his hips into my belly.

Oh ...

We hurried out the door, with Jet pausing to swoop up my postcards. As soon as we reached Bessie, Jet had me pinned against the van, kissing me down my neck.

"I haven't showered, and I smell so bad," I whimpered, fumbling with the door lock.

"You're still honey and coconut and all you. Hurry," he pleaded.

I slid the door open and gave Jet a push on his chest. "Inside, now."

He grinned as he jumped into the van, heading straight for the bed.

I slammed the door shut after me, checking all the curtains were closed before I whipped his AC/DC tee shirt over my head. He paused with his zipper, his eyes going straight to my boobs as I took off my bra.

"Keep going!" I waved impatiently at his crotch. "Pants! Gone! Now!"

But Jet didn't hurry. He slowly slid across the mattress and closed the distance between us.

"Seeing you in real life like this?" His fingers brushed against the side of my breasts, and my skin pebbled all over. "I didn't think I would ever get this chance again."

Jet cupped my jaw and devoured my mouth with his, pressing his body against mine, and then, just as abruptly, he pulled away. "Right now, I want to fuck you so fast and, at the same time, go as slow as I possibly can."

"We have all the time," I murmured. "I'm not going anywhere."

He grinned and nodded, his eyes glassy.

"I, Ariane Wilde, promise you, Jethro Cummings, that I'm here to stay. I want you to be a part of my new life."

"Teaching," he blurted.

"How did you—"

"Debra," he admitted, cringing.

"Fucking hell, Mum," I muttered, swaying forwards to lean against his chest. "It was meant to be a surprise."

"She was always talking about you whenever she was in

the pub. It was torture. But I hung on every word while you were at the cattle station and not talking to me."

I gently pushed back to meet his gaze.

"I'm so fucking proud of you, Ari. You found what you want to do, and you'll be great at it."

"Found out who I want to share that with, too," I murmured.

"Yeah?" He stroked my cheek.

I shrugged one shoulder. "Met some random at speed dating. Promised me a decent shag."

"Did he now?"

"Maybe he'll take me to see his place."

Jet grinned, gently pressing his body into mine, his arousal obvious. "This has been the longest fucking speed date in history, Ari. I'm going to call Guinness World Records to stake a claim on the title."

"Mum's cards worked." I kissed him, barely ghosting my lips over his. "I fell in love, one question at a time."

EPILOGUE

Jet

Sweet or Spicy: Who is your favourite book boyfriend?

Riding a motorbike for twenty minutes with an erection is a special kind of torture. Convincing Ari that she should drive another twenty minutes to see my place was worth the pain.

Ari was right behind me in Bessie, parking in my driveway. And now, facing the front door, with her at my side, key in the lock, I started to panic.

"Just ... wait. Right there." *Fuck, she was really here.* "Don't move."

Would she like my place? Was it clean?

"Can I come inside?" she called.

Checked the fruit bowl—ugh, the banana was more black than yellow. Chucked it. "Nope! Just. Wait. A little longer." Wiped the bench. No flies. Good.

"Can I come in now?" Ari laughed from the front door.

"Soon, very soon." Covered the dirty dishes with a tea towel.

"Meow."

"You have a cat?" Ari shrieked.

"Reluctantly."

"You never told me!"

"Turned up the day after you—"

"I kinda broke up with you?"

Ari was now at the kitchen door, with the cat wrapping herself around her legs.

"Yeah." I gripped the kitchen bench.

"I'm sorry."

All I could do was nod. Ari was an apparition. A fantasy. "Are you really here?"

Surely I was dreaming. I'd made up the whole thing at speed dating and then making out in her van, and then deciding to take things to my house. All a big dream and I would wake up any second.

Ari crossed the kitchen to stand before me. "I'm really here. I promise."

"For good?" Ari flinched. "I'm sorry. I didn't mean—"

"I am here for good."

I clutched the benchtop with a white-knuckle grip. If I let go, I would pull her to me and—

"You're not making this fair," she murmured, breaking me out of my head.

"What do you—"

Ari ran her fingers down my arm, and I shuddered, my resolve weakening.

"These biceps. And forearms. First thing I noticed about you walking into the speed dating night. And now you're just over here flexing your muscles as if they aren't my catnip."

I held up a hand, and Ari's touch retreated.

"Jet, if you don't—"

"I do. I have wanted this for ... longer than I want to admit. Actually, no. I do want to admit. Since I watched your van drive off, I've missed you. I've wanted you. And now you suddenly drive up, and you're back in Ballydoon, and now in my kitchen."

"You're worried I'll drive off again."

"What if I'm not enough? What if this shack, that damn stray cat, Ballydoon—what if it's not enough for you?"

"I saw most of Australia, and the only thing I wanted to see was you again. All I know is right now, I want to be here with you. Nowhere else. No one else."

"I've never wanted any other woman like I want you."

"Then why are you holding onto the cabinetry when you could be touching me again?"

I finally let go and swept her into my arms, fusing my mouth to hers.

Mum always said that home was where Dad was, moving from place to place for work. Ari felt like home; my fingers in her hair, my lips on hers, tongue tangled with hers, our bodies tight against each other.

And that was terrifying. If she didn't—

Ari suddenly broke off the kiss, and I almost fell forward at the loss of her. But she threaded her fingers through mine and squeezed her hand.

I surged towards her, but she backed away, hand on my chest. "What's wrong?" I whispered, aching at what her answer would be.

But Ari's cheeks were pink. She sucked her lips. She looked ... embarrassed? "Jet, I haven't showered in two days."

"I don't care."

Weirdly, it was true. Ari didn't smell bad; sweat, deodorant. Just one whiff of her and it had brought back memories of our bodies wrapped around each other in her van, our skin slick with sweat, how she'd cried my name when I'd entered her the first time.

My dick twitched at the memory.

Settle, Wonder Dick. Settle.

She tugged on my hand and led me through the kitchen.

The hallway.

Towards the bedroom. Blood headed south so rapidly that I was lightheaded. My erection hadn't diminished since she walked into the pub but now I was hard as steel and Wonder Dick was threatening to rip apart my jeans and host a reunion party with the woman who'd been the star of all my sexual fantasies for nine months.

Ari stopped at the bathroom door, and I almost ran into her. "I need to shower," she whispered.

Right. Slow your roll, Jethro.

"I can get you a towel and—"

She kissed me silent, and within seconds, I had her against the doorframe, legs wrapped around my waist.

A roll of my hips had her moaning.

My jeans zipper was right against the heat of her underwear.

Shit, I'd waited nine months to see her again, hold her, kiss her. And I could wait until Ari had showered and felt comfortable. "Sorry," I groaned into her neck and then inhaled.

Don't know what she was worried about. Seriously Ari was the best thing I'd ever smelt, tasted, licked.

My dick now hurt against my zipper, like it was doing everything it could to bust out of my clothes.

"Why are you sorry?" she asked breathlessly, kissing my temple.

"Mauling you," I answered against her jaw. "When you want a shower." I pulled back slightly, a little dizzy from the high of her. "A towel. I'll get you a towel."

Fresh panic washed over me. Shit, what was the state of the shower? The toilet? The sink?

"Let me give the bathroom a once over."

I let her slide down the doorframe, down the front of me, and I stifled a groan.

Bathing was overrated, right?

With a grunt, and hoping I was discreet with how I was adjusting my dick, I checked the toilet—clean, halleluiah! Sink—quickly wiped it down with a face cloth to get rid of toothpaste smear and some shaving hairs. Shower ... a little spot of mould in the grout that had grown back in the last week. Maybe I could give it a quick spray and wipe—

"Jet."

Ari's hand slid up my spine, and I turned around.

Fuck. Double fuck.

All thoughts of cleaning mould were forgotten. She was naked. Her clothes in a pile in the doorway. Her body was more tanned, familiar and new all at once.

"Shower with me."

Ari, thirty seconds before

JET WIPED over the vanity sink, grumbling as he then gave the shower tiles a hard stare like they personally offended him. He was about to reach for a spray bottle of bathroom cleaner.

I made quick work of losing my tee shirt, skirt and

underpants. I had not driven five thousand kilometres and an extra twenty minutes to his house to get back my man and have reunion sex to be then cock-blocked by bathroom cleaner. Time to escalate the situation.

"Jet." I reached out, sliding my hand up his spine.

He gave a little groan, arched into my touch, just like a cat, and turned to face me. The way his face blanked out, and then his eyes sparked with lust.

"Huh?" He grunted, his gaze sweeping over my naked body.

I really would have liked to have seduced him properly, turning up in clean clothes and lacy underwear, but when in doubt, being naked had got his attention.

"Would you like to join me for a shower?"

"Ugfgh."

"Or I could get dressed again and leave you to clean the tiles?"

That sprung him out of his daze. His rough hands seized my waist and pulled me against him. "Tiles can wait."

I smiled against his lips. His jeans needed to come off. It couldn't be healthy how blood flow was so constricted down there.

"Please say you'll stay here tonight." Jet's voice was full of need.

"I'll wake up beside you."

I would do whatever it took to convince him I was here for good.

Maybe a blow job in the morning. Wake him up with my lips around his dick, taking him right to the back of my throat. Make him come so hard he'd have to wait a while until he could get out of bed and walk.

"I'm on birth control, and I haven't been with anyone since you and I were clean after I broke up with Wes."

His Adam's apple bobbed several times before he found his voice. "Are you ... you saying you want me to fuck you bare?"

"If you want to. No barriers."

He nodded slowly, mouth slightly open like he was dumbfounded.

"I want you to hold me up against those tiles and fuck me against the wall. I need you, Jet."

We fumbled with his jeans, his dick jutting out obscenely.

"Hello, Wonder Dick. It's good to see you again, too," I crooned. "You're free now from denim prison."

His penis twitched just before I took his length into my hand and stroked him. Jet's eyes rolled as his head lolled back, his hips jerking in reflex.

I'd barely touched him when his hand wrapped around mine, stopping my rhythm.

"Shower," he rasped, his voice like barbed wire.

Both naked and under the hot water, I expected that he would take charge with sexy times, but instead, he reached over my shoulder and took his shampoo, lathered up my hair and gently kneaded my scalp.

I groaned, needing to lean against the tiles. "This is my first shower with a man."

His hands paused in my hair, and then he spun me around to look me in the eye. "Really?"

I nodded, suddenly shy again.

"Then I'd better make sure you're all clean. Be thorough."

"Thorough?"

"Hmmm," he hummed in my ear and then spun me back around to wash out the shampoo. "All the nooks and crannies."

I laughed and wiped the shampoo suds from my eyes. "Nooks and crannies?"

"How's that for dirty talk?"

"To be honest, that was—ohhh."

His hands, slick with body wash, cupped my breasts and squeezed. My nipples were already puckered but somehow became impossibly hard peaks under his attention.

Wonder Dick poked against my butt cheeks, a constant reminder he was ready. I pressed against him, rocking my hips, but he wanted to make this moment last. As did I.

Jet did as he promised. His hands roamed all over my body, over my breasts, down my hips, my thighs, and back again, soaping me up.

One hand slid up my neck and gently squeezed my throat as the other slid between my legs.

Grasping for the top of the shower stall, I wrapped one leg around the back of his knee as he ran two fingers along my entrance, teasing me. I couldn't move, his hand wrapped in a chokehold around my throat, his lips on my neck, sucking.

"You like that?" he groaned against my skin, clenching my throat slightly.

I nodded, moaning, and then my knees buckled as he slid both fingers inside. My body trembled at the intrusion. I was desperate for more. He nipped down my neck and withdrew his fingers to get more soap to wash my breasts for a third time.

"Jet, please," I whimpered, grinding my butt against his dick. His hand around my throat squeezed slightly, reminding me he was in control.

But I could beg. "Please, fuck me and make me come."

He growled and spun me around, picking me up and

slamming me against the tiled wall, my butt resting on a safety grab bar fixed to the wall.

"Barely hanging on here, Ari. Won't last long."

"Then make it hard and fast, and we can take our time in bed."

He lowered me down, and the blunt tip of his dick parted my pussy lips. "You ready?"

I nodded, and he pushed up as he let me slide down to take him all in. I went cross-eyed at the sensation. Jet, bare, inside me.

Hot water blasted one side of our bodies as he took control of our rhythm, holding me against the tiles as he pumped up. His biceps and forearms corded with muscle, his neck, too. So strong. His tatts crawled under the strain as the water rushed over his skin.

This was fucking, screwing.

We were grunting, panting, skin slapping, grunting like animals.

"Want my hand around your neck while I fuck you in bed?"

His thrusts were sublime. I could barely speak. "Y-yes." I moaned as my walls fluttered, betraying how much his words turned me on.

"Pussy feels perfect, Ari."

"Magical Vagina and Wonder Dick," I managed to say. "What a dynamic duo."

He held my gaze as he swivelled his hips up. "Yes, we are."

His pace was almost cruel. I gripped his shoulders and buried my face into his neck, his breath hot against my skin.

"Oh shit," he gritted out. "Ari, I can feel you're close."

I could only moan his name in reply.

"Fuck, babe. I am about to explode. Need you with me."

He lowered one of my legs, tightened his grip on the other and slipped a hand between us, finding my clit.

I cried out and Jet resumed his pace.

"Hold on, Ari. I'm going to fuck you so hard you won't be able to stand."

"Jet!" I panted. His fingers circled my clit, pressing against those nerves with every thrust. "Oh God, Jet!"

I fell apart. I was sure every atom of my body separated under the hot rush of water.

The pleasure was blinding. I was nothing but light and sensation and waves of heat. Jet cried out my name, and he pulled his hand free between my legs and gripped my butt as his body jerked, pouring himself inside me.

I slumped against him, barely breathing. "You did it," I slurred.

"Huh?"

"That orgasm broke my standing muscles." I patted the safety grab bar. "Thank goodness your grandfather installed this."

"I can't believe it survived that onslaught," Jet muttered, kissing my neck. "You're really here." Another kiss. "You're real."

"I'm here." I managed to hold up my head and cupped his jaw, making him look me in the eye. "I'm really here. And I'm not leaving you."

BONUS EPILOGUE

Jet—three years later
Getting to know each other: Where do you see yourself in the future?

Ari gave me a quick wave from the side of the stage in this massive convention centre room.

She was graduating from university today. Had the full robe, no. Gown? And the hat thing. Cap, I think. With a tassel that kept swinging in her eyes.

Team Wilde went wild as Ari crossed the stage when her name was called out. Bachelor of Education.

"Ms Wilde's fans are indeed wild," the academic chap commented as she took her degree.

"That's my girl," Debra sobbed, wiping the corner of her eyes. "A university graduate. The first Wilde university graduate. My goodness."

Ari had done it. She had her degree to become a teacher.

Five hours later, we walked into the dining room of the Ballydoon pub for our celebratory meal.

Sam, a local photographer, took photos of Ari in her

gown and cap beside the old fireplace. I was going to frame one of these photos and hang it on my wall. Maybe near my fireplace.

Cody strode over, his daughter perched on his arm, and slapped me on the back. "She did it. Ari freaking did it."

"She did," I replied, not taking my eyes off her.

How lucky was I that she chose me out of everyone, anyone, in this country?

"And congrats on your champion sheep."

"Reserve Interbreed Champion Ewe," I said automatically.

One of my best ewes won the Reserve Interbreed Champion Ewe last week at the Stanmore Show.

"Heard you beat the Turners. That's no easy feat. Weren't they like reigning champions for two decades? Did you get a trophy?"

Cody made everything sound like we were talking about pro-ice hockey league like in Canada.

I straightened. "It was seventeen years. And a ribbon."

Tom had been a great mentor these past three years, and I had so much more to learn. After a lucky buy of a stud ram with good blood lines at the annual sheep sales, combined with lots of Tom's advice, I'd successfully bred ewes for the last two years. Even sold a few rams and made good money.

Tom had looked just as happy as I had when I'd been presented with the Interbreed Champion ribbon. And I'll make even more money with the livestock I had from a champion ewe.

The last three years hadn't been easy. I'd ridden a roller-coaster of emotions with the birth of the first lamb on my property, as well as the first lamb death. Digging a hole to bury lost lambs because of a freak storm was harrowing.

But I'd stuck it out. And having Ari with me had made it easier to keep getting up at dawn and doing my best.

"A ribbon?" Cody scratched his chin. "Like a beauty queen sash?"

"Yep."

I couldn't help smiling. Ari had asked me to wear the Interbreed Champion sash to bed that night and, of course, I'd complied with my woman's wishes but now couldn't get the crease out of the word 'champion'. Guess we'll always have a permanent reminder of how we celebrated my win. It was hanging proudly on the mantle over the fireplace at home.

To think that three years and four months ago, Ari drove back into my life, storming a speed dating night to, as she puts it, get back her man.

She stayed at my place for a week, in my bed, before we both admitted we had to surface for groceries and to see family. She moved into the spare room as a flatmate paying me board but had spent every night in my bed since.

My house was just as much hers now.

The shell she posted to me from Darwin still had pride of place in the middle of the mantlepiece over the fireplace.

And she got a place in a university course to study education remotely. Did four-week teaching placements thousands of kilometres away in Far North Queensland. But we made it work. We were the champions of long-distance relationships.

Cody slapped my back, breaking me out of my thoughts, and walked off, saying something over his shoulder about his daughter needing a potty break.

"She's a cute kid," Ari piped up.

Kids. Would we have our own family one day? I smiled,

really liking the idea of having a little Ari and Jet running around our house.

Ari leant in. "How about later, when everyone has gone home, we celebrate today, and I wear the gown and cap and nothing else?"

I groaned. "You know I won't say no to that."

"You could wear the champion ribbon again."

I chuckled as my phone pinged with a text. "Blake says he's on his way. Says congrats to the uni grad and sorry for running late. And, wow, he's bringing a woman along."

"Well, well. Blake and a plus one. Do you know who?"

"No idea. News to me."

"Never thought I'd live to see Blake coupled up."

Just then, Ari's phone pinged with her email alert. She frowned at her screen. "It says ... shit."

"What?"

"Department of Education," she whispered.

"Open it."

"But what if it's a rejection? What if I've been offered a job in the middle of nowhere?"

"If it's a rejection, you'll apply for more jobs. And if it's in the middle of nowhere, I'll visit. You'll visit here in the school holidays."

"We have a plan," Ari murmured, her thumb hovering over the email app icon.

We had talked late in the night many times about what we would do if she got a job far away, if she didn't get a job close by, or at all. Job markets were fickle. But we could make it work for forty weeks of teaching, no matter where she was.

"We've done long distance before, Ari. We are champions of long distance."

She offered me a smile, and I leant in for a quick peck. "Now, open it."

She clicked the app and paced in front of me as her emails downloaded. She selected the first one, her eyes rapidly scanning the words. "Oh my God," Ari whispered, clutching my shoulder.

Long distance would be okay, I reminded myself. We are champions of—

"I've been offered to teach year two at Ballydoon Primary. I start in six weeks."

"Holy shit, a local job? You serious?"

I read over her shoulder: *We are pleased to offer you a teaching position at Ballydoon Primary with year two. Attached are your superannuation and induction documentation.*

"Holy shit," I said again. "You're really going to be here. Right here."

"No long distance required." Ari grinned. "Told you, I'm here to stay."

A BONUS EXTRA EPILOGUE

(Because you're worth it, dear reader!)

Jet

Deal breaker: What are your thoughts and beliefs about marriage?

Twenty-two pimply faces stared back at me.

After two nights away from Ari in Sydney catching up with Theo and Lily, seeing his security business and a bit of shopping, I'd arrived at the place that had changed my life.

Shearing School was in session.

Theo was running the show and had just introduced me for a short speech to the group of lads who'd arrived yesterday.

A bloody speech.

For the longest five minutes of my life. Ari got up in front of twenty-five year two students each weekday and taught them things. But me, in front of twenty-two teens who'd been through the courts, this was a lamb-to-the-wolves situation.

"Let me break it down for you," I began, smoothing my notes. "Everything I owned used to fit in my motorbike's panniers. And I mean everything. Clothes, swag, socks, jocks, stuff. The lot. Even a bottle of cologne, which might sound weird, but I liked the brand, and it always worked with the ladies, and yeah, I have cologne."

The teens snorted and smirked.

"All my music, audiobooks and photos were via an app on my phone. Still are. But now? I have a suit. And three bloody ties. And dress shirts that needed ironing. A wardrobe now, full of clothes and shoes. I even own slippers to wear around the house in winter. And a dressing gown. You feel like lord of the manor walking around in your slippers and dressing gown, listening to the radio, making a coffee at dawn.

"And still have jocks, socks and the same cologne. But now I also have a coffee table covered in photo albums. My, ah, girlfriend, she prints them at the end of every year, choosing her favourite photos, uploading them and ordering a photo book."

I cleared my throat. "And yeah, that's a difference; I have a girlfriend now."

Laughter rippled across the group.

"And not just a coffee table; I now have tablecloths. Placemats. Artwork from the 1970s."

"So what?" someone at the back piped up. "What's your point, mate?"

What even was my bloody point? I'd had one a week ago when I'd written my speech notes and then practised every day in front of Ari.

I shifted in my seat, the fabric scratchy, much like my grandad's old couch. After a year of putting up with its scratchy synthetic upholstery, I realised I could use some of the money I'd scraped together to buy a new one.

My new couch had a chaise lounge to stretch out. Lying on it, in my dressing gown and slippers, drinking hot chocolate with the fire going in winter, I was a king.

Lord Jethro of Kingsley, the name I'd given my property. Named after my grandfather.

Ari had bought me a sign for the front gate for Christmas.

I coughed to clear my throat again. "That's pretty much the question. What is the point of what I'm talking about? What is the point of being here?"

I scratched my head and stared out at the pimply faces. Some of the guys had dull eyes, glazed over. I was either boring them to tears or that was the look of kids who'd checked out, who'd seen things. Shitty, terrible things.

One or two sneered, as teens did, cynical at the world. What the hell did I have to tell them that could help?

But the majority of the teens were listening. Waiting. A little scared about the two weeks to come, mostly curious. And hopeful.

"I guess what I'm trying to say is you're not here to choose tablecloths or new couches or slippers. All of that is just stuff, but for the first time in my life, I like being in one place and having roots. Having friends. Finding love. I even enjoy work. It's bloody hard, and often, but I love getting up at dawn and seeing what the day brings.

"I'm here to say I'm grateful. This place turned it all around for me. People like Theo who challenged me to get on the shears and give it a go.

"I can absolutely say that giving this a go changed my life. And it can change yours if you want it to. You could be cynical and say 'Whatever, man. I don't want a place with tablecloths, and fruit bowls and photo albums and the world's biggest TV.' Fair call. What I mean is, this place could set you up for a different future. Gives you skills and contacts to earn good money that could mean you could get your own place where you feel safe, where you are loved, where you have a fucking fruit bowl if you want to; you know what I'm saying?"

The group laughed again. Some nodded.

"While you're here, do it for you. You're not doing this for a judge or an arresting officer. You have a choice. You're worth it." I quickly folded my speech notes and stowed them in my back pocket. "Any questions?"

One teen threw his hand up, grinning. "You gonna marry your girlfriend?"

The group laughed and sniggered.

My hand flew to the front right pocket of my jeans.

"Look at him blushing. Reckon he's got it bad," one said in the front row.

"Pussy whipped," his mate beside him muttered back.

Happily so, I thought, patting my pocket.

"Settle down, you lot," Theo yelled, hands on hips.

And they did. Then again, Theo was huge and looked like he could squash any of them with his pinky finger.

"In answering your question, one day I will."

That brought on a whispered chorus of oohs, and Theo yelled again for them to knock it off and for final questions.

None, thank goodness. I was off the hook. Done and dusted.

Outside, Theo clapped me on the shoulder, grinning like a proud dad. "Good job in there."

I sighed. "Forgot two pages of my speech. Had my notes in the wrong order."

"Didn't matter. It was great. I mean it. One day I'll convince Blake to do a talk."

I snorted. "Fat chance of that."

"Maybe I'll get you here for a week. Show the boys how it's done."

"Maybe I will," I said, surprised that I meant it.

"Better go back in, and Jet, good luck with Ari ... and it."

My hand flew to my front jeans pocket again. It's still there, you idiot.

Theo just grinned. "Let me know when she says yes. And I expect a wedding invitation."

He winked and strode off before I could correct him.

My phone buzzed with a message from the very woman we'd just spoken about.

Ari: I'll be home late. Got to dash to town before the shops close. Hope your talk went well

Me: I survived. Theo said it was good

Public speaking had left me covered in cold sweat. I patted my pocket again. "I'm not nervous," I muttered, jumping into my ute and slamming the door. "It will be absolutely fine."

Two hours later, I swung around the corner of my road to find a real estate agent hammering a 'for sale' sign at the front gate of my neighbour's place. I slowed the ute, lowering the window, and gave the man a wave.

"Going on the market tomorrow," the agent called out. "If you're interested, you'd better get in quick. I've had off-the-market enquiries already."

The old MacDonald place had been empty for over a

year. The property was slightly larger than mine at sixty acres to my fifty, had two dams that never went dry and had more creek frontage. Previous owners used to run cattle on it, and maybe I could diversify and do that or expand my flock.

The cottage on it was a bonus, and there was an old shed and an old blacksmith's lean-to with an old forge.

"I expect it will go quick," the real estate agent hedged, whacking the for sale sign one more time with his mallet.

I nodded, sucking on my lips, trying not to appear too keen. "That's fair. How much do you reckon it's worth?"

The agent flashed a calculated grin with an actual gold tooth. He said a dollar range, and I inwardly cringed.

The agent sized me up, and the state of my ute, and narrowed his eyes. "You reckon you're in the market, do you?"

I shrugged. "Maybe. Good to know what the value of small landholdings are on our road. I'm next door." I pointed towards my house.

"You thinking of selling?" The agent didn't wait for me to answer, shoving his business card into my hands. "Give me a call anytime. I'd love to give you a market appraisal."

"Thanks?"

"Well, I'd best be off. Open for inspection next weekend. Maybe I'll see you."

Open house? Great, then more people would know, and then more offers.

"Yeah, maybe I will," I said to his back.

I stared at the figure on my banking app while stirring the bolognese sauce in the pot.

The number was a decent amount. Precisely the amount

of money Ari insisted she pay as rent for the second bedroom since she moved in.

Not that she had ever slept in there since she'd moved in. Ari mostly used the room to study, and now prepare her lessons and do marking and store an incredible amount of craft things for small children to use in the classroom. There were more glue sticks in our second bedroom than in an office supplies shop.

We had separate banking accounts, and we split the cost of groceries and bills, but we had one bed. At first, my bed, and now ours.

Definitely ours.

We bought sheets together on sale. New pillows. So many throw pillows. Little useless pillows that Ari says 'adds to the cottagecore aesthetic of the house'.

Whatever that meant. But she loved it, so I did too, even if taking them off every night to go to sleep was a bit of a pain.

Speaking of throw pillows and bed, where was Ari? After two nights away, I missed her. Sleeping alone really sucked.

Bolognese was simmering in a large pot, and I'd just put the water on the boil for pasta when Bessie puttered up the side of the house, and less than a minute later, Ari bounded through the back door, bags swinging from each of her shoulders and in her hands.

"I want details of your talk. And dinner smells great."

She had her blonde hair pulled back into a bun and was wearing her glasses, something new after getting her eyes checked last year.

Ari, as Miss Wilde, year two teacher, with her hair in a neat bun, peering at me through those glasses, had me hot for the teacher every time.

My shoulders sagged. "I forgot to say two pages of my notes."

Ari dumped her things on the kitchen table and came over, wrapping her arms around my neck. "You said Theo said it was okay, but did you think it went well?"

I shrugged.

Ari studied my face and then smiled. "You still don't think you should have been a guest speaker."

I shrugged again, wrapping an arm around her, not quite looking her in the eye. "Felt weird, you know? How many of those guys would ever be in my situation, inheriting a house and property? Couldn't bring myself to say my late grandfather left me a house in his will."

"No fourteen-year-old inherits a house. Your story can help them to make a choice now to learn shearing and hopefully that means their lives will be different."

I managed a small smile. I don't ever think I'll stop feeling like an imposter. But I wouldn't swap the way Ari was looking at me right now for anything, like I was the king of her world.

"I bought you a small cake to celebrate doing your talk," Ari added and then left a light kiss on my cheek.

I abandoned the bolognese and boiling water and backed her up against the kitchen table, shoving one of my knees between her thighs and kissed her hard.

Finally, I pulled away, pleased I'd messed up her bun a little and skewed her glasses.

"You went all the way to town to buy me a cake?" I whispered against her earlobe, giving her a nip. "There's a bakery in Ballydoon, you know."

"I-I know," she breathed as I traced my tongue along her neck. "Wait, stop. I can't think while you're doing that."

I huffed but complied, keeping my hands at her waist and my leg between hers.

"I spoke to a real estate agent yesterday."

I blinked. "Oh?" Whatever she had been about to say, that hadn't been my guess.

"And I ducked into town to speak to the bank today. About buying a place."

"Oh." My hands dropped away from her body, and I took a step back, shifting my feet. "Oh."

"Jet." Ari straightened, and I met her gaze. "About the old MacDonald place next door." I blinked again, and Ari shook her head, laughing. "Your face. You thought I was moving out."

I rubbed my chest. "For a split second there, you had me."

Ari bit her lip, her eyes darting to her tote bag. "I thought about how you'd always said buying next door would be a good investment, and you'd run more sheep. Or cows."

"Cattle," I murmured, my lips curling up.

"Cows, cattle. Whatever. And that having the extra house might mean having a tenant." She rummaged around in her huge bag. Banking brochures spilled out along with a notepad with numbers scribbled over it and the word 'repayments'. Then Ari held up a fist, something clearly inside. "I thought now I'm working and earning some money finally, that maybe I could buy it and then ... we could ... join it together."

She was trembling. "Are you okay? I know mortgages and banks are nerve racking, but is anything wrong?"

"Just nervous." She smiled weakly.

I cupped her cheeks, stroking her soft skin with my

thumbs. "Fuck, what's wrong? Something happened at work?"

Ari gently pulled my hands away. "No, nothing like that. Not at all. I mean, I held back talking to a parent, but that's fine, and I was supposed to cook dinner tonight but the bank—"

"Holy shit, dinner."

I spun around and switched off the gas. Thankfully, I hadn't burnt the spaghetti sauce to black sludge. The water had just come to the boil. Pasta could wait.

I turned back to find Ari down on one knee. "Babe—"

"Jethro Cummings." She beckoned me back to her with a curled finger, and I complied. She grabbed my left hand and squeezed. "I need your attention, please."

"You've got it, Miss Wilde." I frowned. "But, babe, you can stand if you want."

"No. It's not how it's done."

"What—holy shit."

My heart rate sped up like I was running a marathon. *Holy shit.*

Ari flashed a grin, and then bit her lip and nodded.

"Holy shit," I muttered again.

"Jethro Cummings, I meant it when I said I wanted to join the properties together, but I also meant join us together. Like joint bank accounts. Joint mortgage. Make us official."

"Like ... marriage?"

Ari swallowed hard and uncurled her fist, revealing a small black velvet bag. "Yes."

"You got me a ring?"

"Yeah, it's a bit different." Ari sucked on her lips. She was still very nervous. "Ordered online from Broome. I thought it would be a good ring for you because it was in Broome where I realised I loved you."

I grinned like a maniac. Every time Ari said she loved me felt like a gift. The love sceptic had fallen for the goofy shearer.

"Then I love it," I rasped.

Ari swiped the corner of her eye under her glasses. "You haven't even seen it."

"I already know it's perfect." Ari huffed and puffed, and I gently kissed her on her forehead. "I'm not kidding, babe. I know it will be the most perfect ring to make me officially your fiancé. You gonna open that little bag in your hand?"

Ari upended the bag, and a silver metallic ring with a creamy white square and a tiny inset diamond fell onto her palm. "You once told me your favourite colour was the creamy white of wool."

I nodded, my throat blocked.

Ari brushed her finger over the ring. "This here is mother-of-pearl from Broome."

"So it's shell?"

"Yeah, and this style is called a signet ring. Made of platinum. And I thought the colour was like wool, but shiny. And it's a real diamond."

Holy shit. "I love it," I murmured. "Told you it would be perfect." I held out my hand, a slight tremor obvious from nerves or excitement. Probably both. "Put it on me, babe."

"Is-is that a yes?"

"Yes, Ariane." My voice had dropped and was rough. "Make me your fiancé."

Ari dropped the bag, and her hands shook too as she tried to get the ring on my finger. We both laughed, and I seized the moment to kiss her quickly, the action melting away our nerves, and she slipped the ring smoothly over my knuckles.

"Perfect fit." *How had she worked that out?* I held up the ring, letting the mother-of-pearl catch the light. "I have a new favourite colour. It's shiny pearl white from now on. Wool is second."

Ari let out a shuddering breath. "Now I don't know whether you're marrying me for my future property portfolio or for me alone."

I stilled. She was still trembling and rambling now. My love sceptic was nervous as hell.

"Oh God, Jet. I didn't mean anything by what I said. It was a dumb joke. A really lame one, actually. I've been reading too much Regency romance lately involving heiresses."

"I know you have. Found your latest Kitty Malone book. You read the filthiest things." I reached for my jeans pocket and found the little box I'd been carrying for two days. "And you've been bingeing Julia Quinn's backlist because I know the next season of *Bridgerton* is coming soon and you love it. And I also know I'm competing with Jonathon Bailey and Regé-Jean Page for your affections."

Ari laughed weakly and sucked in a breath. "I'm ruining this moment with my dumb comment."

Silently, I pulled the box from my jeans and held it between us.

She sniffed and wiped a tear from under her glasses. I ached to touch her, but I was going to draw this out, make sure Ari really wanted this, and for her to know just how much I wanted this, too.

"W-what's that?" she whispered.

"Ordered this after your first year of uni and have been paying it off. Picked it up in Sydney while at Theo and Lily's place. Was going to wait for the right moment." I closed the distance between us, forming a cocoon of our bodies around the little black box. "And this is the perfect moment."

"Ordered it at the end of my first year at uni?" Ari straightened, frowning. "But that was just over four years ago."

"Yep."

"So what is it?"

"Open it and find out."

Ari fumbled with the jewellery box, almost dropping it.

It popped open, and a silver lioness on a silver chain stared back at her, its diamond eyes winking under the pendant light in the kitchen. A small loop of string also lay across the pendant, and I lifted it off.

"Took me a while to find a silversmith who made this kind of thing. It's a lioness, in case you—"

"I know." Ari's voice cracked, and she smiled, her eyes shining. "You remembered what my name meant."

"My badass lioness, how could I forget? For my badass fiancé."

"Jet," she breathed, one hand flying to her lips. "Are the eyes made of diamonds?"

I nodded. "And you'll have diamonds on your ring, too. When you pick out the style you want."

I held up a loop of string. Ari's brow creased.

"This is to measure your ring finger for your engagement ring." I held up my hand, letting the light reflect off my signet ring. "What about a pearl with diamonds? To match mine? I'll get you a pearl from Broome if you want."

"You really want to marry me?" Tears streamed down Ari's face.

"Yes," I croaked. "Forever." I pulled her into my body, needing to touch her, to remind myself this was real, that this was happening. "I want to share mortgage stress with you." Ari huffed a wet laugh. "I want to open a bank account with you. A Mr and Mrs account. I want to file tax returns together. Organise throw cushions on our bed for as long as you'll have them. I promise you forever."

Ari let out a big sob, and I crushed her to my chest. "You waited so long for me," she spluttered.

"But you beat me to pop the question."

Ari laughed against my collarbone and then leant back to look me in the eye. "I had to. To show you I believed in us," she whispered. "Believed in our future."

Over her head, something flapped in a slight breeze. Since quitting the bar at the beginning of the year, the postcards she'd sent me from her road trip were now on a corkboard on the opposite wall of the kitchen.

In the lounge room next to us, the shell she'd given me was still in the centre of the mantlepiece.

I loved these things. But when it came down to it, none of these things mattered.

Rings didn't matter. Jewellery didn't matter. Not fruit bowls, tablecloths, or this house, or next door if we weren't successful with an offer.

None of it.

Everything I needed was in my arms.

I grinned, the happiest man in the world.

"Like I said, babe, all those years ago, longest speed date ever. And all of it was worth it to have forever with you."

THE END

Keep reading for a bonus chapter of Ignite, book one of the
Fiery Hearts of Ballydoon.

STAY IN THE LOOP WITH LOUISA'S RELEASES AND NEWS:

Sign up for Louisa's newsletter and you'll receive free book promos, the stories behind the stories and latest updates on the world of Ballydoon.

Follow Louisa on her Amazon Author page and social media: Facebook, Instagram and occasionally on TikTok.

Keep reading Louisa's stories set in Ballydoon in Kindle Unlimited. The Fiery Hearts of Ballydoon features a family of rural firefighters trying to save their historic sheep station from the bank while hunting an arsonist before it's too late.

To download your copy, use this handy QR code:

READ MORE BY LOUISA:

Keep reading Louisa's stories set in Ballydoon in Kindle Unlimited. The Fiery Hearts of Ballydoon features a family of rural firefighters trying to save their historic sheep station from the bank while hunting an arsonist before it's too late.

To download your copy, head to the series page here.

Here's a sneak peak of Ignite, the first book in the Fiery Hearts of Ballydoon series:

IGNITE

1

STACEY

Ballydoon Community Group:
     Ryan posted 5:27 p.m.:
  Brigade fire truck headed to grass fire north of town. Presently no danger to property. Close windows and doors for smoke.

GIVEN a choice between watching a movie or being pit crew for Turner's Racing, I'd choose petrol fumes and revving engines every time. The commentators at Walston Park Raceway announced the drag race semi-finals were about to start. I grinned as the crowd roared.

My best friend Sam wrapped her arm around me, bumping her hip against mine.

"Miss it, Stace?" Sam asked.

"A little," I shrugged, tamping down the adrenaline pulsing through me. "Okay, a lot."

When Uncle Bruce had called earlier desperate for pit crew, Sam and I readily agreed, ditching our plans for pizza and Netflix at Sam's house.

A female race driver strutted past with her pit crew. Her

silky-smooth hair and make-up were flawless, and her suit was covered in US company logos: an international competitor. She posed against her car as the official race day photographer took photos.

"That could have been you. Stacey Turner: drags and sprints champion of Australia." Sam wrapped her arm around my shoulder. "Actually, that was you at sixteen. Junior champion."

I snorted. "Don't recall the US sponsorship deals."

"You totally could have got them. You were the best." Sam scowled at the photographer. "And I could take better photos than what he's doing." Sam popped her gum. "Ryan should fix your race car to get it up to spec again."

My old race car was rusting away under a thick layer of dust in the machinery shed at home.

"My brother and I don't have those sorts of funds. Or my uncle."

I'd be lying if I told her I didn't want to get behind the wheel and compete again. But that wasn't going to happen anytime soon. Ten long years had passed since I'd competed in a race event. Now I just pretended, driving the farm ute around the paddocks as if I was on the track.

I pushed aside thoughts about international drivers and a career that never happened as a call came over the loud-speakers: *Drivers for the drag sprint semi-finals need to proceed with your crews to the marshalling yard.*

Our driver, Phil, drove a 1989 Chevrolet Camaro IROC-Z painted black, with red stripes on the driver's door, and covered in decals of *Turner's Car Repairs: let us take care of your wheels.*

Sam let me go with a sigh, glancing around the crowd, her gaze zeroing in on me.

"What?"

"You know, this is the perfect place to pick up."

I rolled my eyes. Sam was perfectly dressed as pit crew and was getting looks from several men. Skin-tight leggings, a fitted tank top with a plunging neckline, her hoodie unzipped, her ponytail swept under a bright purple Turner's Racing cap.

I dusted the front of my wool coat and rearranged my scarf, and caught Sam staring.

"Now what?"

"I thought you were going to change into something more, well, ah …"

"More *what*?" I knew what she was going to say, tucking a stray hair under my woollen beanie.

I'd dressed for warmth, not for male attention.

"Well, to be honest, something slutty." Sam grinned.

I groaned.

"You promised you'd end your sex drought before we got home," Sam continued. "Since we chose here over Netflix and pizza, the universe has offered you a chance to hook up here at the track. You could have changed into the new, hot clothes you bought only days ago."

I'd been in Brisbane for the last two weeks seeing medical specialists but found time to buy clothes on sale or from vintage shops. But the duffel bag I'd brought to the track was packed with dirty laundry, toiletries and a cotton dress.

Sam waved a hand up and down my front. "Stace, you look like you're cosplaying a sofa."

I sighed. "I wasn't going to wear leather pants with the exhaust fumes and grease on track."

"What about leggings? Show off your legs and that arse, girl."

"My leggings are covered in snot, thanks to my three-year-old cousin. I've nothing warm to wear other than what I've got on now."

"You could have done a load of washing last night instead of talking on the phone!"

"Ryan was worried about Charlotte's high fever, blocked nose and a cough." Being an almost-qualified enrolled nurse, I often helped my family with health issues. "It was too late to put washing on after our call."

They were the reason we'd been called to be pit crew. Thanks to engine trouble today, Ryan and his best friend, Benji, were stuck at our farm fixing Ryan's ute.

"For a mechanic, Ryan has the worst maintained car in all of Ballydoon. But ..." Sam paused as she applied lip gloss. A couple of drivers walked past, giving her a look-over. Sam smiled back. "I'm not complaining about Benji and Ryan pulling out today. There are heaps of hotties here. You could still pick up. Just as you wanted to. Operation End-The-Sex-Drought."

"I don't think tequila shots make a binding promise to have sex."

Me and my big mouth. It had been so long since I'd last had sex. I'd made a drunken decree that I'd find a random guy and have sex before I returned home after my medical appointments. Once we'd sobered up, Sam called my drunken promise 'Operation End-The-Sex-Drought'.

I had one night left—tonight—before I was due back home.

I rolled my eyes.

Sam narrowed hers. "Don't you dare back out. Ryan isn't around to scare off any interested men, which makes this a golden opportunity."

As much as I loved my brother, he used his tatts, height

and strength to intimidate anyone who showed interest in me, and it scared them off every time.

Lordy, I wanted to have sex again.

Good sex.

No. I wanted to sleep with a man who knew how to have *great* sex.

Sam seized me by my shoulders. "Repeat after me: 'I am not Rapunzel in the tower. I am not Cinderella in the cellar. I am not waiting for a prince to rescue me.'"

I rolled my eyes again. "I am Stacey on a sheep station and we do have a cellar."

"Oh my god, focus on getting laid!"

Sam released me as I took a deep breath.

"Fine." I slipped my hand into my coat pocket and squeezed a folded piece of paper hidden in there. My heart skipped a beat at what this piece of paper meant for my future.

"I want to get laid. I promise you this girl is rescuing herself. I don't need a prince. Are we good now?"

And, more importantly, she's getting herself a new future when she gets home. My stomach fluttered.

"Yes, we are. When Phil's done for the night, we'll hit up the food trucks."

"Ugh, Stace? Sam?" Phil, our driver, groaned behind us. "I don't feel so good."

Sam and I both turned just as he clutched his stomach, his face turning green.

"Uncle Bruce! We need a bag or something!" I yelled, grabbing Phil's race helmet.

My uncle walked over, keys in hand for the support van to tow the race car into the pits. Ten cars were ahead of us, waiting for the call to proceed for the drag sprint semi-finals.

Phil staggered to the bushes at the side of the track as Sam opened the van's back door. I tossed his helmet into the van and scrounged around for something—anything—to help him. All I could find was a reusable plastic shopping bag, which Phil snatched from me just before he was sick.

Sam, Uncle Bruce and I collectively shuddered. I grabbed a bottle of water from the esky, ready to hand to Phil.

"We're racing in just minutes, and I mean literally five minutes tops," Uncle Bruce said. "Phil, can you drive? It's the semi-finals, mate!"

Phil did a thumbs up. For a couple of seconds, I thought he was okay but he clutched the bag and was sick again.

"Dunno if I can drive, Bruce," Phil whimpered.

"Do we forfeit or something?" Sam asked.

My fingers twitched.

Just this once.

I wanted to grip a race car's steering wheel again. My heartbeat spiked.

The race was, like, ten seconds tops. It would be a crime not to race it, really.

Phil hovered near a bin at the marshalling yard entrance, drinking the last of his bottled water.

I held out my hand to Uncle Bruce for the support van's keys.

"Hook up the car. We'll race today."

My uncle surrendered the keys. "Not sure why we're bothering. He looks bloody awful."

Uncle Bruce moved towards the Camaro as a track marshal yelled for cars to line up for the semi-finals.

I threw the keys to Sam, who caught them in surprise. "You drive the support van," I said. "Hey, Phil! Let's get ready!"

"Stace, I feel terrible." Phil said, tossing his empty water bottle into the bin, before he climbed into the van, rubbing his stomach.

I pulled down the van's back door as Sam buckled up in the driver's seat.

"You're not going to race. Take off your suit," I said, throwing my beanie at Phil's chest. "I'll drive the car in the semi-final."

Phil's eyes widened as Sam whipped around. "But you haven't—"

"I know it's been a while!" I snapped. Adrenaline coursed through me again.

A marshal came to Sam's window, telling her to move ahead. She turned the engine on and drove forward five metres.

"Are you seriously doing this, Stacey?" she said over her shoulder. "We could forfeit and all go home, you know. Or ... head to the bar and pick up."

Phil's eyes rolled back, and he let out a sob.

I took a deep breath. "I just ... I really want to do this."

Sam swore under her breath. I watched through the van's windscreen as the international driver got into her Mustang, ready at the start grid.

"I need this," I added as Sam moved forward another three metres.

"You and your needs," she muttered. "Tonight was about a different need, not this." She waved a hand towards the Camaro and the start grid.

I ignored her and poked Phil in the arm.

"Phil. Phil!" He squinted at me. "Get the suit off. I'm driving in your place."

"You're what?"

"Phil, close your eyes!" I toed off my Ariat boots,

followed by my jeans, coat and tee. For May, it was unusually cold. The car's interior was not much warmer than outside. My skin tingled with goosebumps, dressed only in a long-sleeved thermal shirt, bra, panties and socks.

Phil scrunched his eyes shut, his hand on his stomach. I nudged him in the shin.

"Get that suit off before you are sick all over it!"

With eyes shut, he unzipped the suit down the front and peeled it off, leaving him in a tee shirt that said *'It's not a mullet, it's a mud flap'* and satin boxer shorts. I felt nothing, zip. Zilch. Phil was like a bonus brother to me. He'd met Ryan on the first day of school and they'd been friends ever since, even working together at Turner's Car Repairs.

My mobile beeped. I retrieved it from my back pocket. Ryan had sent several texts.

> Ryan: How's Phil doing? Got a callout for fire. Truck coming for me and Benji. Ute still not fixed.

> Ryan: did a post on the Ballydoon Community Group re fire too

For a population of 958, the majority of Ballydoon residents were on social media, especially active if there was a bushfire threat.

> Ryan: Charlotte getting snuggles with Nanny. Her cold is a little better *attached photo*

I opened the image. Mum had taken a selfie of Charlotte asleep on her lap. But I didn't focus on the cute photo. I was focussed on one word.

Fire.

Fire had been our family's adversary for more than one

hundred and seventy years, since the first James Turner settled in Ballydoon. Since our great-great grandfather founded the brigade with others more than one hundred years ago, our family have always since volunteered as crew.

> Me: a fire? but it's going to frost tonight

I took a deep breath. *Don't let the fire be bad,* I thought as I slipped on the racing suit and zipped it up, cringing at the smell of Phil's cologne.

> Ryan: a grass fire. Should be fine

I exhaled with relief and ignored a pang of guilt as I sent another text.

> Me: All good here. Semis about to start.

> Ryan: heads up, Sunday fam dinner. Amanda is dialling in for a family chat. And Lily too.

Something was up. My older sister, Amanda, only rang us occasionally for Sunday night dinner. And getting my little sister Lily on a family phone call was hard since she lived in Nashville for her country music career.

> Me: Stay safe. Hugs to Charlotte. Sure re dinner. Got to go. About to race.

"What am I going to wear?" Phil whined, his eyes still closed. "I don't have any spare clothes."

"My jeans should fit. And my tee. But not the coat, I need that."

His eyes flew open as my jeans hit him in the head. "I can't wear chick's clothes."

I stuffed my mobile into my coat and then stashed my coat and duffel bag behind the passenger seat.

"It's that or a dress, Phil. Now, give me your driver ID wristband."

He complied and I slipped it on my wrist as Sam glanced back.

"Can't believe what you are doing, Stace," she mumbled.

"Me neither." I pulled my cowgirl boots back on. Unfortunately I didn't fit Phil's racing boots and my Ariats were the only shoes I had.

"Didn't know you had clearance for racing again, Stacey," Phil grunted. "Good on ya."

I paused, unable to respond. A thin sheen of sweat broke out on my forehead despite how cold it was. A thump on the back of the van startled me into action.

"You ready Phil?" Uncle Bruce yelled.

Phil groaned again and I nudged him with my boot to get moving with my jeans.

"Ah, yep, give us a sec," I answered back, deepening my voice. I ran my shaking fingers over the wristband and took a deep breath. Ten years was a long time between races. This race was a far cry from mucking around doing sprint starts in the farm ute in the paddock.

Sam looked over her shoulder. "Got three cars in front of me, Stace. Last chance to not do this very stupid thing."

I grabbed Phil's helmet. "I'm doing this."

"You're an idiot. But you're my favourite idiot." Sam said. "Go and own that track, babe."

I grinned and pushed the helmet on. "You bet I will."

Uncle Bruce thumped again on the back door.

I grabbed my forgotten beanie and threw it again at Phil,

who'd finally pulled on my jeans and tee. "Wear this and don't be sick on my jeans, okay?"

Phil curled up on the floor of the van and made a sound that I took for a yes. Sam threw him a look of disgust. "Don't you dare spew in the car!"

I slammed the visor down on the helmet and opened the back door.

Uncle Bruce stepped back, looking me up and down. He stopped at my chest.

Ah, boobs. Hadn't thought of that.

I crossed my arms and shrugged.

Uncle Bruce stroked his moustache, then shook his head. "I don't want to know." He opened the Camaro's driver's door for me. "Come on, *Phil*," he said too loudly.

I strode to the car, slipped into the driver's seat and gripped the wheel. My heart hammered against my ribs. I closed my eyes and focussed on my breathing. *One, two ...* I'd practised breathing techniques with each hospital visit to prevent terror from overtaking me. *One, two, and three.*

My heart rate slowed and my body zinged. Racing made me feel alive. *How had I left this for so long?* The roar of the crowd flowed over the car like a wave. The commentators discussed the drivers' stats for the race before me. I stared out the windscreen towards the start line. I wanted to go fast. I wanted to win.

"You're up next," Uncle Bruce said, propping an arm on the open driver's window. "I hope you know what you're doing."

I slid up the helmet's visor. "I've got this."

I swallowed hard. This wasn't speeding along a dirt track between sheep paddocks.

Too late to pull out now.

Uncle Bruce nodded and I slid down the visor, about to wind the window up when he spoke again.

"You were the best driver I've had, Stace."

He gave my helmet a pat and a thumbs up, then disappeared to the back of the car.

I wound up the window as Sam towed the car to the start grid. Uncle Bruce then unhooked and pushed the Camaro alone to the start line. The official gave me a thumbs up as my tyres nudged the line. Another with a clipboard eyeballed my wristband and gave me another thumbs up.

Holy fuck, I was doing this!

I eyed off the lights for the start of the race—nicknamed the Christmas tree—red at the top, amber in the middle and green below.

"Green means go," I murmured.

I started the car, revved the engine and zoomed off the start grid to warm the tyres. They gripped the track well. I licked my lips as I reversed back to the start. The other driver took off from the start, his tyres squealing, his car pulling slightly to the right.

I focussed on the finish line. I was ready as I'd ever be.

We waited for the Christmas tree to light up and count down the start, the rumble of our engines drowning out everything and everyone. My heart pounded against my ribs.

Red.

Deep breath in. My fingers grasped the steering wheel. I pumped the accelerator. The engine roared again.

Amber.

I exhaled. suddenly remembering the words Dad had whispered to me before I'd won the junior drag race championships.

"Everything in life comes down to the next ten seconds," I murmured.

Green.

I slammed down the accelerator and hurtled towards the finish line.

Want to keep reading Ignite? Download your copy here.

ABOUT LOUISA DUVAL

Louisa Duval produces and hosts podcasts, and has worked in secondary education, marketing, and is a former journalist. She lives between the city and thirty-five acres of serenity in the Granite Belt region of Queensland with her family and a fat cattle dog-Kelpie cross. Her local rural fire brigade at Ballandean inspired her to start writing romance.

Louisa was shortlisted for Queensland Writers Centre's *Publishable* and *Adaptable* programs with *'Ignite'*. She came second in Romance Writers of Australia's Spicy Bites *'Machines'* competition in 2022 with her short story *'Vintage Love Machines'*. She was also published in Romance Writers of Australia's 2021 Sweet Treats *'Chocolate'* Anthology with her short story *'Chocolate and Orange'*. The anthology won the Australian Romance Readers Association's Members Choice Award for Favourite Romance Anthology in 2021. She was a finalist in the 2023 RWNZ KORU award and a finalist in the Australian Romance Readers Association's annual awards in 2022 for best banter/dialogue, and best short/category romance story, and in 2023 for best banter and best romantic comedy.

By Louisa:

The Wilde Sister Duet:

Book One: A Very Wilde Ever After

Fiery Hearts in Ballydoon series:

Ignite

Embers

Flames – coming in April 2024

Inferno – coming in June 2024

Fiery Hearts (Books 1 – 4) Boxed Set – coming July 2024

Whisky and Sunshine – a prequel to the Fiery Hearts series set in Scotland

My True Love Gave to Me – A sweet Christmas anthology

Worth the Risk – a collection of sweet and steamy short stories, some award winning, set in Ballydoon

To buy her stories, follow Louisa on Amazon here.